DOUBLE ILLUSION

Earth — four hundred years from now — a rotten society in which mankind is doomed to die out — and one seemingly average man with incredible I.Q. potential . . . An ultra-intelligent computer is built and used to govern humanity — and all corruption in the world is eradicated. Mother Machine decides what's best for her human children — and it is done. But the all-powerful computer is turning mankind into zombies. The world's only hope lies in one outlawed, not-so-average man . . .

PHILIP E. HIGH

DOUBLE ILLUSION

Complete and Unabridged

LINFORD
Leicester

First published in Great Britain

First Linford Edition
published 2011

Previously published as *The Mad Metropolis*

Copyright © 1966 by Ace Books, Inc.
All rights reserved

British Library CIP Data

High, Philip E.
    Double illusion. - - (Linford mystery library)
    1. Computers and civilization- -Fiction.
    2. Science fiction. 3. Large type books.
    I. Title II. Series
    823.9'14–dc22

    ISBN 978–1–44480–535–2

Published by
F. A. Thorpe (Publishing)
Anstey, Leicestershire

Set by Words & Graphics Ltd.
Anstey, Leicestershire
Printed and bound in Great Britain by
T. J. International Ltd., Padstow, Cornwall

This book is printed on acid-free paper

1

They disposed of Cook by the simple expedient of crowding him against the emergency door of the bar, sliding it open behind his back and pushing him into the street. They then shut the door in his face and re-sealed it from the inside so that he could not get back. The entire operation took only eleven seconds and no one noticed. The operators were pleased with their success, not to say a little smug. They had been paid a *Purple* each for the job and it had been child's play. Too often they had been paid a couple of *Reds* for a nasty one which had to be undertaken under the noses of the Nonpol or virtually in the regular patrols of the legal police, and those sort of jobs were risky indeed.

This one, however, had been so easy and so casually committed they felt almost innocent. After all, they hadn't actually killed the man, not directly, anyway. All they had done was to

1

maneuver him into a position where his chances of survival for more than an hour were unlikely in the extreme. As he had at least nine hours before he could hope for any help, his demise was a foregone conclusion.

Perhaps, fortunately, the four executioners were not thinking men. It never occurred to them to ask why they should have been paid so much to dispose of a ninety I.Q. Prole who was exactly the same as the seven hundred other Proles employed by the Combine.

Cook didn't know either and was in no position to think about it. For several seconds he was mentally and physically paralyzed with terror. He thought of beating on the door and shouting that he was outside, but he knew that before anyone heard him the noise would attract attention — the wrong kind of attention.

His only hope was to stand absolutely still and pray for a miracle — only he didn't believe in miracles. All Cook believed in were facts, and the facts were that he was out in the street at night. No one went out at night unless in an armortaxi or, if rich, in a fast hypnad flyer.

Cook, himself, had never left the Combine since first being employed there at the edge of eighteen — why should he? The giant block contained his place of employment, nine hundred cramped living cubicles, and all the recreation facilities that science could provide. There were gymnasiums, parks and, with hypnad techniques, a blazing summer beach complete with swaying palms, dreamy lagoons and Atlantic rollers.

Generally speaking, a Prole lived, mated, procreated and died in the block. An intelligence quota of only ninety seldom asked or desired more. This was a pleasant, secure and gently regulated life, and few had the ambition to step beyond it.

In these pleasantly familiar surroundings Cook had left his cubicle and descended by the gravity shaft to his favorite bar for the customary evening drink. There, for no comprehensible reason, he had been crowded against a door which should have been sealed and pushed into the street. Now, persons unknown, perhaps quite unaware of his predicament, had re-sealed the door with him on the outside.

Cook rated his chances of receiving grievous bodily harm at a conservative one hundred and fifty percent, his chances of survival at an optimistic two. If he survived, hospitalization would be painful and protracted.

He didn't move, apart from his eyes and an uncontrollable twitch at the corner of his mouth; he stood perfectly still against the section of the building which was now an undistinguishable emergency door. Sweat trickled slowly down his face, but he had enough self-control to confine his breathing to near silence.

One never knew what was out there or what kind of devices were alert for such minor signals as the respiration of the lungs, the beat of the human heart or the chemical processes of sweat.

Above him the building which he had just left soared upwards until it was lost in shadow, and before him stretched the street.

It was a brilliantly lit thoroughfare — a mile-wide river of non-reflecting blackness, yet somehow dwarfed by the soaring buildings on either side.

A street where one stood as naked and as visible as a black fly on a sheet of white paper — *Oh God, Oh God, what am I going to do?*

From the opposite side of the street, a red light flashed on and off like a beckoning, be-ringed finger.

A woman? Perhaps he could make her apartment and stay there until dawn? Hope died within him almost as soon as he had thought of it. In the first place he'd never get across the street, and, in the second, a woman who could afford a call-light would regard his meager supply of green exchange with the contempt it deserved. She was after bigger game, the wealthy wolves, the prowlers and the psychos, who could afford to risk the night in hypnad flyers.

Police caller? No. The nearest one was just visible nearly a mile away at the beginning of the next block; he'd never make it.

5

Cook stood there, trying to reason his way out of an impossible situation and knowing he couldn't. Worse, this was not new; from all accounts it happened quite frequently. A man offended an overseer or an exec or fell down on his work quota and was summarily tried and expelled. Then there were those rare young ones — usually hopped up with lift-pills — who, out of bravado or stupidity, thought they could break the block and survive in the city at night.

His own case was, of course, unique, but the result was the same. The psychos *knew*, they knew that perhaps eight or nine times a night someone was thrown out and they patrolled the streets, waiting.

No one worried about a Prole. They were the outcasts of the new feudalism, the nightmare of the politician, the barrier to economic recovery, the burden of the privileged classes. It had not come to pogroms or mass extermination yet, but it had been talked about and was getting very close indeed.

The Proles! Six billion labor-class entities who, with an average I.Q. of only ninety, could not be fitted into the structure of society, who had to be carried by a sagging, groaning economic structure already on the verge of collapse. What the hell could you *do* with them? Anything they could do the machines could do six times as fast and twenty times more efficiently. No wonder, despite government subsidies, the Combines often lost patience and tossed some of the burden into the street.

Anyone found dead at dawn was immediately written off as an accidental death without further enquiry.

Cook thought of these things as he fought off a mounting hysteria. The desire to move, to tear himself away from the closed door, was almost overwhelming. He wanted to run and keep running; he wanted to scream and keep screaming. *Oh God, I've got to hold on!*

What for? What good would it do? He would never hold out until dawn, and, even if he could stand still for nine solid hours, something would find him long before that.

Nonetheless, he continued to stand

there. A shadow against the wall, an outline of a human being in the standard, ill-fitting one-piece proletarian suit with its round black collar and indicative yellow arm bands.

He was a target, a specimen, a butterfly to be pinned down and made to twitch by the first psycho who spotted him. That was the trouble with psychos, although they lived in a world of fantasy, when it came to exercising their particular perversion they wanted the *real thing*, and hypnad variants wouldn't do.

Cook never knew what made him look up — perhaps his terror had awakened new perceptions — but suddenly he raised his eyes and, almost at the same moment, the voice came whispering down at him.

'*Oh what can ail thee, knight-at-arms,*
Alone and palely loitering?'

The voice came from a bat, a black bat circling and spinning between the great buildings high above him.

'*O what can ail thee, little Prole,*
So haggard and so woe-begone?'

The voice was soft, gentle, the voice of a young girl and deceptively compassionate.

Cook was not deceived either by the sex or the compassion; both served to increase his terror, and so did the bat — it had a sixty-foot wingspread.

He made to step forward then changed his mind — what good would it do?

'*I met a lady in the street —* '

Cook put his hands over his ears. Why didn't she *shut up*? *Must* she toy with him, *must* she play cat and mouse? Dimly, behind his abject terror, was a vague resentment that she should parody Keats, of whom he was particularly fond. The title of the poem, however, was appropriate: *La Belle Dame Sans Merci*. Mercy was a word which, he was quite sure, was not included in this psycho's vocabulary.

A red-hot needle seemed suddenly to pierce the calf of his leg and he nearly fell. *Oh, God, it had started!*

He was not burned, of course; the lady was using a psychosomatic weapon which stimulated his brain into *feeling* a burn, but it made little difference. She could still burn him to death without leaving a mark on his body. He thought, despairingly, that she probably would before she had finished with him.

The bat began to descend in slow spirals, drawing closer. He could see the leathery membranes of the beating wings, the hungry, blind, mouse-face. *Oh God, Oh God!*

It was then he heard the sound, a thin wailing moan and, far in the distance where perspective drew the great buildings together, three yellow lights appeared which rushed towards them.

Apparently the lady saw them, too. 'God blast your luck, little Prole, but maybe I would have been kinder.'

Then, apparently, she panicked, for the bat suddenly turned into a giant wasp, which became in turn a burnished projectile and a hawk with outstretched claws before she finally touched the right button and vanished completely.

The yellow lights rushed towards him, the wailing rising to a shriek which filled his ears and numbed his mind before stopping abruptly.

Silence seemed to surge back leaving him breathless and then he was staring at three black vessels poised silently some ten feet above the black surface of the street.

They were — save that they lacked tail feathers — exactly like darts. The kind of darts, he understood, once used centuries ago in some curious and long forgotten game. These darts, however, were thirty feet long and their barbed snouts seemed to point at him with the blind impaling hunger of swordfish.

A voice said: 'Who are you?'

And he answered, shakily: 'My name is Cook — Stephen Cook.'

'What are you doing out at night?'

'I was shut out.'

'Why?'

'I do not know.'

'You are evasive. You must accompany us to headquarters.'

2

One of the black darts descended to the level of the roadway and an opening appeared in its side.

He stepped towards it, legs feeling rubbery and unreal. Out of the frying pan and into the fire — from a female psycho to the doubtful mercies of the Nonpol. What had he done to deserve this?

There was no one inside the vessel, but a seat was briefly outlined as he stepped in. He sat down and the door through which he had entered closed silently behind him.

The vessel did not seem to be moving but he knew it must be. He knew the Nonpol would convey him to one of their interrogation centers, and then — Cook tried to stop thinking about it.

In the darkness he sat perfectly still, but he guessed he was being scrutinized, checked and folder-filed in readiness for the coming interrogation.

His guess was correct. The unseen watchers saw a slim man of thirty with pale but youthful features. They took the routine particulars. Height 5 feet 10, hair brown, eyes brown, chin firm, clefted but not aggressive, nose straight, mouth sensitive — they were already a little bored; damn Prole, sheer waste of time.

The Nonpol, however, made thoroughness and efficiency their watchwords, so they went deeper.

Intelligence Quota (curious), 110, well above Prole level; better try the potential. They tried and whistled softly. They then re-ran their findings to make sure. Intelligence Quota, conscious mind, 110; Intelligence Quota, potential, 612 — good God! They looked at each other meaningfully and called in experts.

The experts confirmed the figures and dug up further facts. Cook's mind was 'rigged'; someone had psyched him shortly after birth and deliberately blocked in certain sections of his brain. The blocked-in area was 'triggered' so that only certain stimuli, physical, visual, mental or hypnotic, would awaken it.

13

The experts didn't know what the stimuli were; they said it would take years of careful testing, and an error would probably prove fatal. It was, they said, like opening an ancient safe with a numeric combination. It was all right if you knew the combination in advance, but if you didn't you could fumble around forever trying to find it.

The Nonpol officers shrugged. Well, since they couldn't open the safe, maybe they could trade it to someone who could, or else find someone sufficiently disturbed by the information to pay good money to dispose of it. Through a variety of agents they began a series of discreetly veiled inquiries, and Cook's folder file began to increase in size. By the time he arrived at the interrogation center, the information it contained was considerable.

Cook realized suddenly that a door had opened at his side and that he was staring into a bleak white-walled room containing a white-topped table and three chairs.

Three men sat in the chairs, blank-faced but youthful-looking men in black

14

tight-fitting uniforms.

'Stand in front of the table.'

He left the vessel and stood there and the opening through which he had passed closed silently behind him, leaving a bare white wall.

'Your name is Cook?'

'Yes.'

'Do you know where you are?'

He hesitated, choosing his words carefully. 'I conclude I am in an office of the Civil and Voluntary Police Organization.'

One of the men looked up. He had a thin, youthful and almost friendly freckled face. His words, however, were anything but friendly.

'So you're smart enough to play it smooth, you Prole bastard, but we are not deceived. You are shivering in your shoes, so you dare not tell us what you think, but I will tell you what you think. You are thinking 'I must be polite or these Nonpol thugs will beat me up.'' He half rose. 'Perhaps you are less polite, eh? Perhaps you are numbered among our enemies and think of us as the Gestap scum.'

'No — no — I — '

'Save it, my friend; you, too, could be misinformed. Therefore, it is time you knew the truth. Modern society is so devious, the law so corrupt, that much injustice and cruelty takes place against which the average citizen has no redress under the present system. The C.V.P.O. was created to protect the average citizen from non-indictable crime — you understand?'

Cook said: 'Yes, sir, I understand,' and tried to look both surprised and suitably impressed, but he was not deceived. The Nonpol was an illegal quasi-military organization which sold itself to the highest bidder. A descendant of the once respected private security organizations, it had degenerated into what was virtually a terrorist society, which, it was rumored, was amassing funds for a political coup and a military autocracy. In the thirty years since its inception the organization had acquired a reputation for brutality which had earned it the title of Gestap.

The organization was, however, extremely clever, and the law had been unable to prove either the brutality charges or the political aspirations of the party's ruling caste. It was, in consequence and as far as the law was concerned, still a security organization with an outwardly respectable, if suspect, 'front.'

The freckled man said: 'How did you get outside at night?'

'I was pushed out.'

'Deliberately?'

'I do not know.'

'But you suspect?'

'It could have been an accident.'

No one moved, but something slapped his face brutally and he staggered. The Nonpol, needless to say, were specialists in psychosomatic weapons.

They looked at him coldly. 'Did something disturb you? You appeared to stagger. Is it because you are evading the issue? That is unwise; we cannot help you unless you cooperate. We know you are not cooperating because we have little telltale instruments which tell us if you are not speaking the truth. Suppose we begin again: you suspected the incident was deliberate?'

'Well, yes, I did.'

'That is better. Have you any suspects?'

'None.'

'And you can suggest no reason for this incident?'

'No.'

'We can suggest some of the reasons. We were in touch with your place of employment prior to your arrival. We understand that you made things with your hands, model ships and things like that. Also that you read and collected printed books, particularly books of verse.'

'My work — '

'Your resident psychiatrist was not concerned with your work but your leisure, and your use of it was regarded as abnormal. Your work's overseer was disturbed by it — would you care to speak to him?'

Before he could answer, the wall vanished and a projected image of Ran Kilburn, his work's overseer, appeared seated in a chair.

'So you have yourself in trouble, Cook?' Kilburn's eyes looked through

18

him and beyond him. 'What is this ridiculous story of someone pushing you outside? There was no trial and no expulsion order.'

'You think I'm stupid enough to go outside at night on my own?' Cook was suddenly angry.

'I think you're curious; I think you're too curious. I think you could have opened the door to see where it led.' Kilburn was still looking through him and refusing to meet his eyes, but Cook sensed he was uneasy. Furthermore Kilburn's words seemed too pat, too assured, as if he had been carefully rehearsed in what he had to say.

'It's not true. I was having a drink and minding my own business.'

'So you say.'

'Consult the bar records when I return; they'll prove I'm speaking the truth.'

'Well — ' Kilburn's small round eyes were suddenly blank — 'well, I'm afraid that will be a little difficult. When I found — when you were reported missing, I filled your post. Naturally, I thought you were dead.'

'But I'm not dead.'

'I can see that, but you are as far as we are concerned. Rules are rules; you didn't report for work and, therefore, you've been replaced. It's not that you've been dismissed; we haven't *room* to take you back.' He blinked moistly and unconvincingly. 'I'm sorry, Cook. It's just us. I'm sure there are quite a lot of other Combines that will be only too glad to make room for you.'

Cook tried to shout: 'You liar, you know damn well — ' But the image flickered and became a blank wall again before he could open his mouth.

He swayed, conscious of a faint feeling, and pulled himself erect with an effort of will. Another Combine. Did Kilburn think he was stupid? In this day and age to be without employment was tantamount to a death sentence; no one wanted an unemployed Prole. The only escape route was labor/adjustment, and that, too, was equivalent to death.

3

The three uniformed men looked at him expressionlessly, then one of them said: 'Want us to take this up?'

'Take it up?'

'Don't be obtuse, Prole, this is our kind of case, an injustice which cannot be remedied through the normal processes of the law. Well?'

'Well, I — '

'How much money do you have? Oh, don't look so blank, for God's sake. Look, to remain an efficient organization we require funds, we charge for our services — clear? You must have received wages, possibly assurance policies — how much can you raise?'

Cook did some muddled and hasty mental arithmetic. 'I have twenty-five greens with me; if I realized on my insurance — well, say two Reds.'

The man nodded. 'Ample. Of course, when you get your job back you become a

21

contributor, you understand that? It's five percent of your earnings; it's a kind of insurance and you get priority in case of need — excuse me.' He left the room.

When he returned some five minutes later he said: 'Get lost.'

Cook stared at him. 'I don't — '

'Do I have to draw a diagram? It's not enough.'

'But you said it would be ample.' Cook was confused and becoming angry.

'It was until your Combine offered us four Reds to forget it. Can you outbid them?'

'No.'

'Then there is nothing further to discuss. We are a business concern. Naturally we accepted the highest offer.'

'You're going to throw me out?' Cook was too desperate now to be over-awed by uniforms. He couldn't go out there again, he *couldn't*. 'Couldn't I stay here until morning? I'll pay.'

The other frowned, glanced at his watch, then shrugged. 'Six hours protective custody will cost you ten greens.'

'I have it.' He fumbled the money from

his pocket. 'Only until light, only until dawn.'

They took the money and counted it. Then they threw him in a cell. The cell had no bed but part of the floor was resilient. He dropped onto it and almost immediately fell asleep; terror had exhausted him.

While he slept, the Nonpol continued with their inquiries. Unfortunately the Mayor could not be contacted, but an anonymous caller bought his life.

'Let him go.'

'We've been offered five Reds to get rid of him.'

'I'll give you a Purple. Set him free and freeze the bidding for two hours after his release.'

'Agreed.'

'You will sign a contract. It will be signed on a time limit — understood?'

'Understood.' They signed the contract and the bank draft. They had to or lose the money. Again, if they dishonored the contract they could not only be sued but would lose considerable prestige at the same time. Consequently the Mayor did not hear of Cook for eight hours . . .

* * *

They let Cook out into a misty daylight and closed the door behind him. They were not kind; they had found him at street level and they released him at street level, and the streets of this age had not been designed for pedestrians.

There was no footpath and he was compelled to edge warily along the wall, ready to avoid any near-psycho who felt a sudden compulsion to brush him off the wall with an adroit swerve. Highways were sacrosanct and any pedestrian who appeared on one was fair game. Desperately he made a taxi signal with an extended thumb, and a yellow checkered cruiser swung swiftly towards him, the side door open.

'Jump! It's forbidden to stop.'

He jumped and was hurled head first into the upholstery as the car accelerated.

'What the hell were you doing on the street?' inquired the unseen operator petulantly. Then briskly and without waiting for an answer, 'Where do you want to go?'

'The nearest bank, please.'

'Four greens — put them in the receptor.'

After a few hundred feet of level travel, the vehicle reached a green official rise-shaft and arrowed upwards to a taxi platform.

'City Corporate Bank, your destination.' The door slid open and he climbed out.

Inside the bank, hypnad projections of well-dressed youthful clerks inquired his business, bowed, opened doors for him and conducted him to the correct department.

His documents were checked, his identity double-checked and then a screen lit behind the hypnad clerk. Figures appeared on the screen and a male voice began to explain the figures with all the inferences but none of the intonations of apology. Sum assured minus two percent risk, minus five percent pre-maturity tax, minus . . .

Cook had paid out three-quarters of his wages since the first week of his employment; of this he received two Reds and eight greens, exactly one tenth.

Stunned, he went into a call box and tried to think. With careful spending, keeping to concentrates and periodically forgetting to take one, he might survive four months. On the other hand, he had to have a place to sleep, which, no doubt, would cut the time in half.

He had no idea of the possible cost but he could call from here and find out.

He found out. The cheapest demanded thirty greens a night, which would eat through his reserve in no time.

He tried hostels. The hostels wanted only a modest five but they required proof of employment. They were not interested in displaced Proles.

With a sick desperation inside him, he continued his inquiries; already the calls had swallowed two of his greens.

Finally he struck lucky. A small transients' hostel was grudgingly prepared to accept him for two nights only. 'The law won't allow more, see? The city won't tolerate flop houses, but any Prole traveling from one Combine to another can break his journey for a rest. It's ten greens and no extras — okay?'

He said, 'Yes,' because he was too desperate to do anything else. Maybe the two nights would give him time to find somewhere else, and, for a limited period, he would be safe at night.

Wearily he made his way out of the call box and found his way to one of the free public express tubes. He had no illusions now, and a reasonably clear picture of his position. A displaced Prole was not only out, but kept out. Either he starved to death, fell a victim to the psychos, or desperation drove him to labor/adjustment.

Labor/adjustment would, of course, find him a job with another Combine. They would also find him another personality with a complete set of memories to go with it. They would change his name, number and tailor him to the particular demands of the labor market. The Combines would then accept him with some little enthusiasm because he would be a Prole-plus — dedicated, conscientious, highly trained and the nearest thing to an organic robot that science could dig up. He would, of course, never remember that he had once been called Cook and had been thrown out of another Combine.

He reached his destination and was checked to see if he had a police record. Then a hypnad arrow directed him down a long, badly lit corridor to a narrow oblong cubicle which so closely resembled a coffin that he protested angrily.

'What the hell!' said the invisible clerk. 'You paid for a place to sleep. You've got room to sleep, haven't you?'

'But look — '

'You want to sleep or walk about?'

'Sleep, naturally, but — '

'Then sleep, Proley boy. Consider yourself lucky; you've got air-conditioning free and, if you can pay, piped entertainment and a caller.'

'But washing, toilet facilities?'

'Straight across the corridor and extra. Cuddle down in your little nest, boy, I'm tired.'

He tried to sleep and almost instantly realized he was hungry. He pressed the 'snack' button, inserted a green, and a packet of protein sandwiches and a plastic bottle of coffee with a sucking tube were ejected from a slot in the wall and fell on his stomach. There was no change from the green, although he calculated he could have bought the same snack in a Combine canteen for twelve whites.

He ate the meal slowly and, although ravenous, was hardly aware of what he was eating. There must be an answer, there *had* to be; he had to find a way out of this situation somehow. No use trying the information banks, they would instantly refer him to labor/adjustment. A lawyer? No, law fees were prohibitive. If only there was someone he could talk to, someone to whom he could explain.

It was then it came to him — an Oracle. Why hadn't he thought of it before — *The Guild of Oracles!* Shakily he pressed the directory button, selected a number at random and dialed the number in the instrument above his head.

As the call connected, one wall of the cubicle vanished and Oracle Stress appeared at his side.

'And what can I do for you, sir!' Oracle Stress was sprawled in a lounge chair and was so grossly fat that Cook immediately decided the man must despise the hypnads. No one would make himself look like that from choice; he must really be like that.

'I asked you a question — well?'

'Sorry.' Cook pulled himself together and began his story haltingly. As he proceeded, however, he found himself speaking quietly and with a wealth of detail. There was something about Stress, personality, genuine interest, a quality which made him easy to talk to and hold nothing back.

Slightly short of breath Cook stopped, realizing there was nothing more to be told. 'Well?'

'I'm thinking about it.' Stress made peculiar gestures with his hands, then stroked his double chin with sausage-like fingers. Since halfway through his story, Cook realized suddenly, Stress had been making those same peculiar gestures.

The Oracle snapped his fingers suddenly. 'Call you back.'

As the image vanished, a voice in Cook's head said: 'Run for your life!'

4

Miles away, City Mayor Maurice Tearling heard the report of the Nonpol with growing alarm.

'Are you sure this alleged Prole has a potential of 612?'

'See for yourself; there's the report.'

'And an anonymous caller paid all that for his safety?'

'Here's the contract.'

'Yes.' Tearling looked at it and tried to smile easily. 'Rather a dangerous man to have around loose.'

'We thought so, too. That's why we called.'

'Quite.' Tearling frowned. He despised and deplored the Nonpol, but probably they were the only organization who could find and deal with Cook.

The caller seemed to read his thoughts and played his cards discreetly. 'We should be most happy to relieve the Mayor of any anxiety concerning this man.'

Tearling fought a losing battle with his

conscience. They couldn't afford the risk; if his potential developed, the man might unwittingly discover certain facts, and they couldn't afford those facts to be broadcast yet. It was expedient that one man should die for — hadn't he read that before somewhere? As for the Nonpol, hell, let them do it. Once The Plan came into operation, they, too, would be deprived of power.

He nodded briefly. 'I must confess I am very anxious.'

The Nonpol officer nodded blank-faced acknowledgment and broke contact. Details and payment would be arranged discreetly later.

Tearling sighed and tried to relax in his chair. It was job enough keeping this business from the Oracles, who already had their suspicions, without having a potential super-Oracle loose in the city.

Six weeks, just six weeks — that's all he needed. After that . . . He wondered suddenly if they'd acclaim him. Well, he and the others — he wasn't in this thing alone.

Of course, if it got out now, they'd

crucify him. There'd be a revolution; all the mayors of all the Free Cities would be lynched out of hand. As for the Restricted Cities, their answer would be simple and direct — war.

'We had to do it,' he told himself, unconsciously apportioning some of the possible blame to the others. 'We *had* to.'

As he had many times in the past four years, he began to justify his actions in his mind. No one could take this life if he stopped to *think*.

The entire culture had the skids under it and was sliding down an icy slope towards the lip of a precipice. The economy was top-heavy and liable to collapse in chaos at any moment. On top of this, the culture groaned under the weight of uncountable unemployables who had to be fed, clothed and housed at the expense of the community. The corrupting influences of the hypnad had worsened the situation even more, blinding men to truth and concealing ugliness under an illusory cloak of beauty. No one knew, or cared, any longer where illusion ended and reality began. Behind the façade of well-being created by the hypnad, crime flourished like weeds in an unkempt garden, and the numbers of dangerous psychos increased daily.

No man, or group of men, could stand this nerve-wracking civilization for long, seeing the entire culture racing downhill to inevitable destruction. When the crash came, there would be very few survivors left to wander around and pick up the pieces. Riots, starvation, and the hysteria bomb would slash Earth's billions to thousands in less than a year.

The Restricted Cities were in no better position. They, too, had been unable to resist the insidious invasion of the hypnad. They, too, despite regimentation, grandiose economic plans, and constant purges, were just as unstable financially. In any case — despite denials to the contrary — they were tied to the Free Cities financially.

It had to be done, Tearling told himself again; someone had to find a solution and call a halt. He, and a few others, had had the courage to make the decision, to act — God, *someone* had to save the race! If he were ever asked to explain, if he were ever called for judgment, he would say that. They would all say it: 'We acted for mankind, we acted to save the race. It is our defense that, because of our actions, the world has survived to judge us.'

Tearling felt some of the tension drain from his body. It was right; he was *sure* it was right.

The Nonpol arrived at the hostel exactly ten minutes after Cook had left.

'Where did he go?'

'How the hell should I know?' Nervousness was making the clerk shrill-voiced and truculent.

'He said nothing to indicate a possible destination?'

'No.'

'You recall every word he said?'

'Well, not every word, but — '

'Then it is possible you may have forgotten something, some chance word, perhaps?'

'I don't think — '

'But you are now not quite certain?' The Nonpol officer sat down on the only available chair and began to pare his nails carefully. 'One can forget consciously, but one never forgets unconsciously. The subconscious mind, like the city memory banks, retain everything, everything you have ever heard, thought, or experienced. I'm very much afraid we shall have to dig it out.'

Pyscho-interrogation damaged certain sections of the mind unless skillfully treated.

'No!' The clerk made a wild rush for the door but stiffened before he got there and fell heavily against the wall.

The officer watched indifferently as his equal attached electronics to the clerk's head and body and began their interrogation.

They got everything, but it didn't do them any good; the man didn't know anything.

Cook's call was checked, and the entire conversation was played back by the city memory banks. There was no evidence of a tie-up between Cook and the Oracle. In the first place, Stress had spoken only a few noncommittal words, and, in the second, he had called back and, receiving no reply, had broken contact.

The officer frowned to himself. It looked simple, but was it? To all intents and purposes Cook had made the call, suddenly lost his nerve and run. On the other hand, where had he gone? A man on the run and terrified by a hostile world does not give up his only haven easily. It seemed damned funny that directly after speaking to an Oracle . . . and you could never tell with Oracles.

The officer had no intention of tackling Stress himself; in any case it was forbidden. Dealings with the Guild were always undertaken by specially chosen men. The Nonpol had bucked the Guild twice, each time with dire results before they had learned the lesson that there was something more dangerous than their own organization.

The officer sighed, looked indifferently at the unconscious clerk, and left the room.

5

Cook had left the hotel in great haste but without undue panic. He knew exactly where he was going and exactly how to get there, but the route was anything but direct.

He traveled six miles by express tube, ducked out at a halt and doubled back two miles by the elevated slide-way. Then, again by slide-way, he headed east for miles and doubled back again, this time by the seated fast-slide.

He had no set plan, but he knew exactly when to change his direction and mode of transportation. He also knew that he had to keep a wary eye open for possible pursuit and to attract as little attention as possible.

He was not a thinking man, but he had a clear, if slightly confused, picture of what was happening. Stress, the Oracle, either believing his story or for reasons of his own, had done a direct hypno on him.

The peculiar gestures he had used while listening had contained a hypnotic instructional pattern. The reasons for such a procedure were reasonably clear; verbal instructions could have been recalled by the city memory banks, but there had been no verbal instructions. There was nothing to connect Cook with the Oracle which could be followed by the Nonpol or, for that matter, the legal police. Stress had got Cook out of an obviously dangerous situation without committing himself. Briefly, Cook wondered why.

Finally, he arrived at his destination, and an automatic door slid open to admit him.

Stress, still in the sprawl chair, looked at him over the huge mound of his stomach and grinned faintly. 'Glad you arrived safely. Do sit down.'

Cook sat, hesitantly. 'I think I'd better tell you I haven't much money.'

Stress blinked at him. 'A naturally honest man — how refreshing.' He sighed faintly. 'Sometimes there are more important things than money. Don't worry. In due course, you'll pay.' He yawned prodigiously. 'I've ordered a meal — I know you must be hungry — after which we must talk; your problem intrigues me. Ah! here we are.'

A ro-serve emerged from the service hatch and placed a meal on a table-tray directly in front of Cook's chair.

The ro-serve looked like an attractive waitress, but Cook knew it wasn't; he had seen ro-serves in the director's quarters back at the Combine. The ro-serve was a machine with an attached hypnad projecting a waitress image.

Cook ate ravenously but his mind was elsewhere, recalling all he had read and heard of these people.

The Guild of Oracles were of the race, but stood apart from it; they were at the service of the people, but did not belong to them; yet they had taken the place of the high priest, the father confessor, the family lawyer and the personal psychiatrist.

True, unlike the city memory banks and the cybernetic consultants, they were fallible, but they were also *human*, patient, they listened and they were wise.

They were the only body, apart from medicine, which followed defined principles, betrayed no confidences and abided by a strict set of rules.

All of the Oracles had an I.Q. of not less than five hundred and were in consequence the virtual supermen of the race.

They embroiled themselves in human problems because they were sworn to help rather than to lead, or perhaps because their intelligence granted them infinite compassion.

Cook pushed aside his empty plate with a sigh and reached for his coffee What was going to happen now?

Stress seemed to read his thoughts. 'Don't look so hopeful. I am an Oracle, not a conjuror. I cannot produce rabbits from a hat until I have a hat. In short, my friend, you are the hat, but before I can produce anything you have to be shaped and made to function. Up to now you have been an organic cog in a huge machine, clothed, housed and fed by the Combine. You have been told when to work and when to play, when to wake and when to sleep, but no one has ever told you how to think. We must teach you that first, then you must learn how to fight and how to kill, how to create and how to destroy, and, more important, how to decide when to do neither.'

Cook shifted uncomfortably in his chair. 'I don't understand. I only came — '

'I know — you only came for advice. But, in the first place, your story intrigued me. In the second, since you have been here, I have had certain instruments in operation which tell me something has been done to your brain. Lastly, and most important, Cook, you are inevitable; you *had* to happen sooner or later.'

'I still don't understand.'

'You don't have to understand — yet.' Stress heaved himself to an erect position. 'Listen, I can turn you loose again, or, if you are willing, the Guild will not only hide, feed and protect you, but educate you for your role in the world.'

'My role?' Cook blinked at him.

Stress sighed. 'Yes, your role. You are a potential Oracle, but — don't let the idea go to your head — *only* if we develop it.'

Cook scowled at him suspiciously. 'In exchange for what?'

Stress smiled and spread his fat pink hands. 'In exchange for your cooperation when developed.'

Cook continued to scowl. 'It's a little vague, isn't it?'

Stress laughed softly. 'Too vague. Why not follow through step by step and commit yourself only as your understanding grows?'

Cook shook his head slowly then seemed to come to a decision. 'When and how do I begin?'

'Now, if you wish — just a little history lesson and some applied thought. For instance, what did you have to eat just now?'

'Eh?' Cook looked at him blankly. 'You saw what I had, steak, vegetables, gravy.'

'Yes, that was my order for you, but did you have it? Remember, room service plates have a controllable hypnad, so did you eat mush with the service hypnad projecting an image of steak — you don't know, do you? You don't even know if I

43

am fat or if this body you see is a hypnad image. You, like everyone else in the world, cannot distinguish illusion from reality, and since nearly everything is illusion, we have come to regard illusion as reality.

'Let me quote an example: you claimed you were attacked by a bat, but had you stopped to think, you must know there is no such thing as a bat with a sixty-foot wingspread. You could have thought further, you could have thought the truth. You knew, but did not consider that you were facing only a psycho woman in a standard flyer. Unpleasant enough, true, but nonetheless a fact. That flyer had a hypnad which by the pressure of a button could project several images of something else, a bat, a hawk, a giant wasp, but every one an illusion — are you following me?'

Cook nodded quickly. Until now he had not considered the implications of the hypnad, but the other's words were making him think about it.

'Ah!' Stress rubbed his hands as if pleased. 'We will now have a brief history lesson on the hypnad. First the technical side: some two or three centuries ago, I am too lazy to recall the exact date, a man named Haelitz succeeded in impressing a mental image on receptive substance called *mecressoline*.

'I will not go into technical details save that, after ten years of research, he discovered a method whereby he could 'play back' the impression. The procedure went like this: Haelitz would sit in a chair and concentrate on, say, an oak tree. The mental activity of his concentration would be recorded by his device — a huge helmet affair — and impressed electronically on *mecressoline* tape. Haelitz would then vacate the chair and invite a volunteer to take his place. This volunteer donned the helmet and then the recording was played back. Needless to say, the volunteer immediately had a strong impression of an oak tree. This experiment was in truth the birth of the hypnad.

'As science progressed and the knowledge of mental activity became profound, it was found possible to 'draw' a mental impression in much the same way it had been possible to 'draw' a sound in the far distant days of the photoelectric cell. At the same time it was discovered that, with a certain amount of electronic jiggling, the projected image could be stepped-up from what had been a purely mental impression to something approaching reality. In short, the mental impression became a hypnotic impression affecting all the senses — the day of the great illusion had begun.'

Stress paused and sipped some water. 'In the meantime, technology and micro-engineering had kept abreast with the developments. Haelitz's clumsy apparatus had been reduced by degrees to the size of the ancient transistor radio, and, finally, to a unit no bigger than a button.'

Again Stress paused but this time to make an apologetic shrug. 'As you have probably gathered, I love the sound of my own voice, but all this is important. Now for the social side.

'As the hypnad neared perfection, it became available to the general public and there the trouble began. Oh, yes, it was used innocently enough at first, display windows, stage shows, small rooms to give an impression of spaciousness, but then it began to spread like wildfire. There was no need for makeup — a hypnad unit could project a picture of a flawless complexion, and, almost in the course of weeks, the fat became slender, the thin, voluptuous, and the aged, youthful. Illusion met with illusion and in a very short time true reality was forgotten. A woman might be ancient, but she didn't *look* ancient and, much worse, she didn't feel ancient if one touched her. A man might suspect he held a crone in his arms, but she didn't *feel* like a crone, and, after a generation, no one suspected or cared.

'There was no getting around this business; even photographic film was treated with *Mecressoline*, so that the developed picture showed the projected image and not the true reality. There are, I agree, a limited number of penetrators in existence, but these are held only by very high and specially selected police officials.'

Stress sighed faintly. 'Consider the repercussions — are the buildings really tall and graceful, or are they hypnad images? Am I wearing a smart suit, or some roughly shaped colorless material with hypnad buttons?'

He moved his body slightly and attempted the impossible task of crossing his legs. 'We know and we do not know, because we no longer care — everything looks good, so why worry?'

He became suddenly grim. 'Few remember that from the hypnad was developed the psychosomatic sidearm, the weapon which strikes at the nervous system and convinces the brain of the body's destruction.'

He made an angry gesture. 'Death-wish guns, curse-weapons — we're living in a half-world of psychotic necromancy and technical black magic.'

6

Cook rose and went towards the window. 'This is a real window?'

'Quite real, this is an old building, and I insisted it remain. There are not many real windows in the city now.' He rose and joined the other as he studied the city.

'And what do you see out there, Mr. Cook? You see a city which stretches as far as the eye can see in every direction. A city of slender and graceful buildings, most of which reach the clouds. The buildings are divided by mile-wide streets, those running north to south are black and those running east to west are white, giving, at a distance, a soothing checkered effect.

'These same streets are packed with gleaming yacht-like wheelless vehicles, while above them the transparent pedestrian slide-ways and the architecture of suspension bridges link the buildings with the fairy unreality of cobwebs — beautiful, wouldn't you say, Mr. Cook?'

Cook frowned at him. 'Well, yes — yes, I suppose so. I've never really thought about it.'

'Think about it now, Cook, think and look.' Something strangely compelling seemed to have crept into the Oracle's voice. 'Don't just accept what you see, ask yourself if it is real and then try and see it as it *really* is.'

'I don't — ' Cook's eyes dilated suddenly.

'Look, *deeply* — '

It was then that Cook put his hands over his eyes, made choking sounds and fell backwards.

Stress caught him deftly before he struck the floor and carried him easily to the nearest chair.

'You had to happen,' he said aloud. 'Sooner or later you had to come along; pray God it's not too damn late.'

Cook regained consciousness five minutes later.

'What happened?' It was clear he had no recollection of having seen anything unusual.

'You fainted, probably strain.' Stress was almost brusque. 'We must get you out of here. It won't be long now before the Nonpol makes a casual call.'

'How will I leave — they're on the watch for me!'

'Oh, that's simple. One or two of them may have penetrators, but they're looking for a brown-haired Prole. You'll walk out of here in a second-class suit; you'll have fair hair and a fair moustache, and I've a little something here which will change the color of your eyes. These people are so enslaved by the hypnads that they've forgotten the art of simple disguise.'

He produced a small box and some phials from a wall cupboard. 'You will be met by a contact; it is all arranged.' He laughed softly. 'Strange as it may seem, there are still parts of this planet which are not city — a jungle or two, deserts, mountain ranges. We have hideouts and strongholds here and there.'

Cook looked at him strangely. 'Why?'

Stress shrugged. 'Clearly, sooner or later, the whole damn situation is going to blow up in our faces.' He frowned.

'Another thing, something is brewing, something is being prepared. We do not know what it is, but we suspect it is highly dangerous . . . '

★　★　★

Pointer, the deputy commissioner, glanced at his watch for the tenth time in as many seconds. 'I wonder how it will start?'

'Oh, for God's sake!' Tearling, the Mayor of Free City Two, was tense and on edge. 'How the hell should I know? We've done what we had to do. We've exactly five minutes to wait and find out.'

'Sorry. It's just that I wish I had an idea.' Pointer relapsed into moody and uneasy silence.

Somehow it was not quite silence for Tearling. He could hear the tense breathing of the others in the room, the thudding of his own undeniably rickety and aging heart. God, he should have taken a lift-pill, anything to ease the tension, anything to stop *thinking*. No use asking himself now if he'd done the right thing; too damn late for that.

His mind began to wander. Never found Cook, had they? Not that it mattered now; too late for anyone to do anything. Strange all the same — people didn't just vanish into thin air, and even with the illusory negation of an expensive hypnad, people could still be found. It was known that the Nonpol illegally possessed some penetrators which would quickly have revealed him.

The Nonpol suspected a tie-up with the Oracles. Probably they were right, but that, too, did not matter now.

Tearling became aware of a curious haze in the room which made the faces of the others blurred and strangely ill-defined.

'What's going on?' He half rose. 'Someone playing jokes?'

'It's coming through the air conditioners.' Pointer's voice was calm to the point of casualness. 'You realize the time, I suppose?' He stifled a yawn with an obvious effort. 'Zero plus, should have started — have I turned everything off!'

'Turned everything off?' The inquiry seemed to move something in Tearling's mind. 'Yes, that was important, let's see now.' He had the curious impression that all over the city people were asking the same question. That slowly, everything was stopping, aircraft operators switching to automatic, ground vehicles slowing, carefully parking, and that all the people everywhere were making sure that all switches were at 'safe' and looking round for a place to sleep.

Sleep? Why sleep? Couldn't sleep now, *particularly* now — zero plus, should have started. Started! No! This wasn't, *couldn't* be — Despite himself, his eyes closed. No this wasn't part of the Plan; the Restricted Cities must have got wind . . . put in a counter blow before . . . so tired . . . gas . . . treachery . . . typical of . . . Oh, God . . . got to . . . to . . . what? He lost consciousness.

★   ★   ★

Tearling awoke from a dream in which he had been swimming in the widest and bluest of oceans and sighed. He was past swimming and cared little for oceans, but

54

the dream had been restful and pleasant.

The Plan! Now what was it? Oh yes . . . yes . . . With some effort he opened his eyes and saw a thin film of dust on the polished surface of his desk. Dust? What the devil was the matter with the auto-cleaners? But of course, he had been asleep, hadn't he? The cleaners wouldn't operate while the room was occupied, but dust — *dust*. How long had be been asleep, for God's sake?

The others were stirring, too, moving their limbs and rubbing their eyes.

'What's been going on, Mr. Mayor?' Pointer was staring almost popeyed at his watch. Then he shook his head quickly. 'Nine days! I must be crazy.'

'Eh? What?' The Commissioner of police sat upright suddenly. 'What's that about nine days?'

Pointer stared at him unseeingly. 'I set my watch for a period check when I began to lose consciousness. It . . . it says we've been asleep *nine days*.'

'Impossible.' The Commissioner made protesting motions with his hands.

'Not so impossible.' A cold feeling of

terror was seeping like liquid into Tearling's body. 'Look at the dust on the desk, the floor, the windows.' Abruptly he touched the caller-surface. 'Get me the Mayor of Free City One.'

Almost immediately a chair and an outline built up beside his own chair.

Lennon, the Mayor of Free City One, raised his hand in salutation. 'I've been standing by for your call.'

Tearling said: 'We've been asleep.'

'So have we — we figure we've been asleep about nine days.'

'Er — yes.' Tearling stared at him. Lennon's hypnad image was of a tall, distinguished man, benevolent, graying at the temples, but Tearling knew he was old, just as he himself was old, although his own hypnad projected an image of dark-haired strength and maturity.

'Two old men,' he thought inconsequently. 'Two tired old men, wheezing behind their Peter Pan masks and united by a common terror.'

The Mayor of Free City One — which had once been called New York — stared at the Mayor of Free City Two — which had once been called London — and both asked the same question together.

'Is this part of the Plan?'

Neither attempted to answer the other, and Tearling said, shakily: 'Is it world-wide?'

'I'm afraid it is. The Restricted Cities are blaming us and threatening God knows what.'

'If this is part of the Plan — they'll learn.'

Lennon nodded slowly. 'Yes, they'll learn. That's the only thing that worries me, Tearling — had we the right to involve the entire world?'

Tearling made an irritable gesture. 'Haven't we discussed that a thousand times? Without involving the entire world there would have been no Plan. With a setup like ours, the Restricted Cities would have descended on us like brigands; they would have devoured us in a matter of weeks. No, you know as well as I, it had to be all or nothing.'

'I know, I know, but it still troubles me.'

'Not so much as nine days uncon-sciousness troubles me.'

'It *could* be part of the plan.'

'Quite true, but I'll be very much easier in my mind when I know for certain — I'll call you back when I have more news.'

The image of Lennon vanished to be replaced almost immediately by another image. This one sat in a straight high-backed chair, wore a drab brown uniform, and glowered.

'I suppose you imagine you're omnipotent?' He spoke *Interlings* in a throaty way with an unnecessary suggestion of accent. 'What, in the name of God, do you think you're playing at?'

Tearling forced calmness into his voice before answering. 'If you would be good enough to tell me what you're talking about, perhaps I could answer you.'

Borrand, Director of Restricted City One, made a contemptuous snorting noise which was very close to a snarl. 'Don't play it cute with me, Tearling; I didn't go to sleep for amusement. In our cities we cannot afford nine-day rests; time is geared too closely to production. You've completely sabotaged our fourth three-year-program.'

Tearling laughed a little contemptuously. 'You and your fiddling little programs — you can no more solve your economic problems than we can.'

Borrand leaned forward. 'Go ahead, jeer. You'd like a couple of hysteria bombs through your roof, perhaps? We could make it a couple of million, enough to turn every Free City into a screaming madhouse. Our fiddling programs are geared for production jobs like that.' Fury seemed suddenly to explode inside him. 'You treacherous creep, with your appeals for peace, cooperation, live-and-let-live; you couldn't even *fight*; you had to hamstring us while we slept.'

7

Tearling stared at him and swallowed, conscious of a sudden 'miss' in the uneven beating of his heart. 'I have no idea what you are talking about. We've been asleep too, you know.'

'So you claim — can you vouch for your technicians? Look, my friend, while we slept and you feigned it, some experts went through our city fast, sabotaging certain industrial plants, gimmicking a lot of war machines and even going so far as to 'rig' most of our transport. Who did it? It couldn't have been an army of your techs conveniently masked against your sleep gas, could it?'

He paused, drew a deep breath, then went on more calmly. 'Listen, Tearling, I'll be frank; we rattle sabres, we shout about living space, we make horrible threats, but it's *a policy*. We didn't *want* war. On the other hand, we don't like provocation, our people don't like being needled and

— again I'll be frank — but for my intervention your damn Free Cities would be knee-deep in hysteria bombs by now. I had one hell of a job stopping other directors clobbering you first and conducting an inquiry later — do I make myself clear?'

Tearling half rose, clutching the edge of his desk shakily. 'Borrand, believe me, I know nothing about this, absolutely nothing.'

The Director shrugged. 'Convince me. You sound sincere, but you wouldn't be a Mayor unless you could put over an insincerity with the ring of truth.'

Tearling said, haltingly: 'If I come — if I come to your city, personally and alone, to discuss this matter — what then?'

Borrand blinked at him. 'You'd do that?'

'I would to avert war.'

'Very well, I'll do my best, but I cannot guarantee your safety. Some of the militia are a little wild.'

'I'll take the risk.'

'Do that and remember that patience is like a fuse — it gets burned away with the passing of time. Don't take too damn long getting here, Mr. Mayor.'

As soon as Borrand's image vanished, Pointer said: 'You must be mad. You're playing right into their hands. They've been praying for a chance like this for years.'

'Perhaps.'

'No 'perhaps' about it. Before you've drawn a breath, they'll have you flat on an interrogation table; they'll suck information out of your brain like water out of a glass — defense plans, economic figures, stockpile centers, then they'll toss your mindless body back for us to look after.'

Tearling sighed. 'Only *one* mindless body, Pointer, not several million. I advise you to study the effects of an hysteria weapon before I return. It might restore your sense of proportion.'

As he went down the corridor some two minutes later, however, he was conscious of a queasy feeling in his stomach. Pointer was right, after a few formalities they'd grill the sense out of him, it was too good a chance to miss. On the other hand, he couldn't risk war, that would be the end of everything.

He approached the door of his private garage which slid back obediently as he neared it and passed inside.

Wearily he approached the official vessel and frowned at it without enthusiasm. Certainly it was impressive, the nose painted with the rondel of the Free Societies, the white star of unity, the mayoral coat-of-arms and several minor symbols, the meaning of which he had forgotten — but all of it failed to stir him. He had the uncomfortable feeling it was going to come back as a coffin.

He climbed in, dialed the flight pattern and pressed the starter panel. His hands were shaking uncontrollably.

Nothing happened.

He swore and tried again.

Still nothing happened, and angrily he switched to the secondaries.

This time there was a response but not from the motor.

A voice said: 'An emotional index has been incorporated in the structure of this vessel. The instruments will not respond because your emotional level is such that you could not operate the vessel with safety.

'As you are no doubt aware, the accident rate at free-flight levels has trebled in the past eight years. It is to cut these terrible figures that an emotional level index has been incorporated in every form of transport.'

'Who the hell are you?' Tearling looked wildly about him. He knew there was no one with him — despite hypnads, the assassin-circuits would have warned him instantly of another person in the vessel.

'Try again when you are calmer,' said the voice.

Tearling did not become calmer, but he tried desperately for ten minutes before he finally gave up in despair.

In the corridor Pointer met him. 'Been gimmicked, eh? I guessed. Mawn tried with the same results. My God, all hell's broken loose — we think we've been invaded.'

'Invaded!' Tearling leaned against the wall, his aging legs feeling curiously weak. 'You'd better calm down and tell this slowly, Pointer.'

Pointer drew a deep breath and tried to force calmness into his voice. 'When you left, and in view of the situation, we thought it our duty to place the city on a war footing, but we couldn't. The launchers wouldn't come out of their housings, the delivery hatches of the stockpiles are sealed, the defense circuits don't respond, and no power on earth can get our robotic troops and flyers moving. We couldn't lift our hats to defend ourselves. As far as defense is concerned the Restricted Cities could march in with bows and arrows and beat us to our knees.'

Tearling shook his head slowly, his mind strangely clear. 'Somehow I don't think they will. I rather think they're in the same position as ourselves — what made you think of invasion?'

'Colonel Payne has been arrested.'

'Arrested! By whom?'

'Two men in white coats like doctors. He was trying to force the doors of a stockpile base. Apparently these two appeared and ordered him away. There was an argument, and Payne tried to draw a weapon but they froze him and led him away. There have been several more unconfirmed reports, more or less similar and by no means confined to this city alone.'

'You're suggesting this is some sort of extra-terrestrial invasion?'

'Why not? Where the hell did these people come from? Who tied our hands as regards defense and where did the sleep gas come from in the first place? The question I would like to ask — '

'For God's sake stop firing questions at me and let me think.' He walked slowly back to his office frowning and feeling a burning resentment inside him. Invasion? No, it couldn't be, and yet — it wasn't fair, after they'd done so much, risked so much.

He dropped wearily into his chair and called Borrand. 'I shall not be coming.'

'We guessed. We suggest you make peace with your God if you have one.'

Tearling looked at him tiredly. 'Don't wave a club at me, Borrand. You can march in now and take over; there's nothing to stop you. Our stockpiles are sealed, circuits dead and our fliers gimmicked. Are the gentlemen in white coats your idea? If so, I find them singularly inappropriate for your kind of secret police.'

Borrand was silent for long seconds, then he said, quietly, 'Right, Tearling — our agents informed us you were in the same position as ourselves but we needed your word to confirm it — any ideas?'

'It has been put forward, tentatively, as an extra-terrestrial invasion.'

'We thought of that, too. It isn't you and it isn't us and, although it doesn't leave much else, a lot of facts don't seem to fit an extra-terrestrial invasion. What about that Plan you've been working on so long?'

Tearling felt himself pale. 'Plan?'

'Don't play it stupid, boy. We don't know what the plan was or how you intended to put it over, but we know you had it and we know you were desperate.'

'I can assure you that this business is no part of it.'

'Perhaps you can and perhaps I believe you, but I still think we ought to hear about it. Much as we both dislike the idea, we're reluctant partners now, both with our backs to the wall. We fight together or go under. I suggest an all-city conference, right now, before our white-coated friends come and drag us away . . . '

⋆   ⋆   ⋆

The conference room, with the aid of projection and hypnad techniques, became a gigantic auditorium with tiers of seats rising upwards from a central rostrum.

No one was present in the actual sense, the crowded seats being projections from every represented city in the world. The delegates could see each other, converse together but in actuality all of them sat in their own offices.

Borrand opened proceedings. 'Gentlemen, there is no need to go into details concerning present events, we all know what they are. Our defenses rigged, our guns spiked and the streets of every city in the world patrolled by white-coated unknowns against whom we have no defense. The scale of arrests by these white-coated invaders grows hourly and none know from whence these people came or what becomes of their prisoners.

'It has been suggested from many sources that these people are extra-terrestrial invaders, but the question must be asked how did they get here and when? They have been checked with penetrators and do not appear to be using hypnads, but hypnad or not there is one peculiarity, they are all the same, *each one is an exact duplicate of the other.*'

Borrand paused briefly and looked directly at Tearling. 'Before proceeding, however, we are all aware that the allegedly 'free' societies had a plan, The Plan, by which they hoped to solve the problems of their decadent and failing communities. We have since learned that, by a peculiar coincidence, the date set for this plan ties in exactly with the beginning of the present crisis. Mayor Tearling has assured me that plan has no bearing on present events, but at the same time he has omitted to state the nature of his scheme or schemes. Speaking on behalf of the entire world I now demand that

Mayor Tearling reveals the nature of this plan not only to absolve himself but to allay distrust and ease the mounting panic which confronts us all in this terrible situation.'

Borrand sat down and Tearling knew he was trapped. To withhold information now would brand himself and all the associate mayors as the instigators of the present crisis. Why had Borrand picked on him? Why not Lennon, Kirby, Kanuko or Spier? They were all in this together.

He rose shakily, aware that his heart seemed to be banging angrily and unsteadily at his ribs. 'Gentlemen, I will make this brief — brief and brutal. If brutality offends, I am sorry, but only a fool denies the truth and a fool is unfit to hold office.'

That ought to shut Borrand up for five minutes, he thought, bitterly, and continued. 'Let us face it, our nerve-wracking civilization was plunging to destruction and, although we deluded ourselves, our plans and programs could do nothing to prevent the inevitable. Desperate, aware of the crash ahead, seeing in it the destruction of the entire race, we took a calculated risk, we gave the burden to a power more capable of reaching the solution than ourselves.'

8

There was silence. Tearling had expected an uproar but there was silence, a kind of strained silence as if those present were not sure if they had heard correctly. Some of the faces had a curious shut look, the kind of look a man reserves for an embarrassing crank, and they refused to look at him directly.

Finally Borrand said: 'What kind — of power?'

Tearling swallowed. It wasn't easy now; he had never visualized an inquiry *before* the event, but always afterwards, at a time when he could point out the benefits already reaped.

He cleared his throat and tried to control his heart, which now seemed to be pounding unsteadily just behind his eyes and in his temples.

'We built a machine,' he said. 'Several machines, cybernetic machines, so complex that the finished units covered several square miles of space. Such machines, built in every Free City, were linked by beam control into a single functioning unit. We fed this unit the problems of our crumbling nature and gave it a free hand in reaching a solution.'

This time there was an uproar. Tearling put his hands over his ears and allowed the muffled noise to surge round him like angry seas.

It went on a long time. Dimly he was aware of someone shouting 'Silence!' and another voice urging the delegates to question in order of priority.

Finally the noise receded and he was conscious only of the shaking of his limbs and the pounding of blood in his ears.

'How would *your* experiment effect us?' asked a voice. He was not sure who asked the question but he knew it was one of the directors — it didn't matter.

Without looking up, he said: 'The machine should have been powerful enough to adjust the selector circuits of all minor cybernetic units throughout the world.' He paused, desperately short of breath.

Borrand's voice boomed at him. 'You tried to hand the destiny of the human race to the decisions of a machine!' It was an accusation.

'It was a step, an inevitable step.' He raised his hands protestingly but even to himself his voice sounded quavery and insincere. It had seemed so right at the time, but now —

'An inevitable step,' he repeated. 'Machines were already controlling our traffic, dealing with supply and construction, and manufacturing and delivering consumer goods without human supervision. It was a logical step forward. We had to do it or go under.'

Someone shouted: 'Traitor.' Waved his fist angrily then hissed, 'Judas — you tried to sell out the race!'

Tearling dragged himself to his feet again and looked at the blurred sea of faces; somehow he felt strangely calm. 'You dare to call *me* Judas?' He stared upwards in the general direction from which the voice had come. 'At least, rightly or wrongly, I was prepared to do *something*. You, my accusers, were prepared to do nothing. You were content to let the world slide to destruction without lifting a finger to stop it — a covey of squawking Micawbers desperately hoping that something would turn up.'

He paused, desperately short of breath, but he was too good a politician to let his temporary advantage slip away. 'The short-sighted policy is all too evident now, with the world slipping away from us. My opponents would have my head for something I attempted but did not succeed in completing. As I have told you, we tried to save humanity by handing our affairs to a cybernetic machine. We did not do this blindly, but only after years of research and experiment. Every step was checked and counter-checked, every possibility and deviation considered and prepared for. *We erred on the side of benevolence. We made certain that the human race would be helped, guided and protected.* Any deviation from that policy would have triggered the safety circuits and destroyed the brain completely.'

He paused, wheezing faintly and faced them unblinkingly. 'I will be frank with you — I am sorry it failed.'

He waited for the words to sink in then smiled coldly. 'When my opponents succeed in proving that the whitecoated invaders, now almost in command of our cities, are the direct result of our attempts to save the race, then I shall be happy to face them.'

He sat down with the comfortable feeling that he had won the day, but he was by no means happy. Problem after problem, there was no end to it, no end at all; it was like trying to push back the tide. On top of it, he felt so damned ill, and the sea of faces kept blurring and tipping sideways in a most peculiar way.

It was then that he became aware of a murmur of voices high up among the tiers where Borrand should be sitting — yes, it was near Borrand. A small untidy man who had evidently forgotten to turn on his hypnad kept imposing himself over Borrand's image. His eyes protruded wildly and he gesticulated frequently. He held something in his hand which he waved directly in front of Borrand's face.

Finally Borrand stood up and there was something in the way he stood which made Tearling's heart flutter painfully.

'Happy, Mayor Tearling?' There was triumph in Borrand's voice but it was subdued, a minor tone in a voice which filled with fear. 'The leading cybernetist in Restricted City One has been studying the invaders. As you are aware, these people are normal even with penetrators, but leading cybernetist Charve has taken photographs using film untreated with *mecressoline* — tell them about it, Charve.'

Charve had his hypnad switched on now and looked tall, dark and impressive. He was detachedly and coldly direct. 'There are no alien invaders; there are no white-coated men exactly alike; there are, however, machines using a new-type hypnad, and projecting a hypnotic image of white-coated men. The machine, as near as I can tell from observation, consists of a combined drive and anti-gravity motor — operated from a remote radio-control center — several camera eyes and, I presume from results observed, a number of non-lethal restraint devices such as psychosomatic paralysis weapons. It looks like this.'

A picture suddenly appeared in the center of the auditorium and Tearling saw a sphere about as big as a football, a glittering crystal football, faceted like a diamond and shining like a star.

Somehow his mind could not grasp the idea, still less the implications. Why? What had that glittering round thing to do with him — with the machine? Why were they all staring like that, accusingly? If the invaders were using remote control devices and hypnads, it wasn't his fault, was it?

They hadn't specified, not directly, how the machine should exercise its function to help mankind. Certainly not with white-coated ... but they were not white-coated men, were they? They were round glittering spheres, round machines floating on an anti-gravity ... machines ... *machines!* No! no, it couldn't be —

Dimly he was aware of falling, of clutching at a desk which he somehow missed and landing jarringly back in the chair.

I'm sick, he thought. *It's my heart. Thank God for the micro-capsule; it will send a warning automatically. Post will soon be here, Post and Myers. They'll know what to do. Will they get here in time? Can't breathe properly.*

He became aware of a numbing sensation in his wrist and the tingling mist of biocardialine in his nostrils. They had arrived — *thank God!*

Slowly his breathing became easier and the mists which swam before his vision drifted away.

'That was a nasty one, Post, I — ' He stopped. It wasn't Post and it wasn't Myers. It was two men in white coats, two precisely identical men, gentle, compassionate. No, no, not men, glittering spheres — machines, not men.

He tried to sit upright but was pushed gently back.

'You must not exert yourself. You have had a severe heart attack.'

He said, desperately, still not fully grasping the situation: 'Don't be a damn fool. Give me a shot to put me on my feet for half an hour. I've got to face those people out there.'

'Such a procedure would be most dangerous. You must rest.'

'Rest! Good God, man, I've been talking about a rest for thirty years and still got by without one. In any case, I can't afford to rest, not now.'

'On the contrary, you can afford to rest and particularly now.'

'Don't talk like an idiot, I've got to stay on my feet. I'm the Mayor. At the moment there's no deputy. Who the hell is going to run this city without me?'

They leaned towards him together, the gentle compassionate faces for the moment seeming to fill his entire world. 'We see you do not understand. The burden has gone — there are no more labors of office nor strain of responsibility. You are free.'

'Free?' Cold blind fingers seemed to be clutching at his heart.

'Quite free. There is no further need for mayors or soldiers or economists or police.'

Tearling, rigid with sudden terror,

understood, but sheer reaction made him protest desperately. 'You don't understand. I'm *the* Mayor; I've got to run the city.'

'Rest, rest. Mother will take care of the city.'

It was then that Tearling suffered a relapse and had to undergo further treatment.

When he regained consciousness some two hours later, however, he felt remarkably fit and almost young. His heart was beating steadily and he was no longer short of breath.

'You feel better now.' It was a statement. 'You may now look forward to many more years of active life. Your heart has been removed and replaced with a mecco-plastic pump; many of your glands were replaced with laboratory substitutes. You may, without exaggeration, regard yourself as a bare forty-five years of age.'

He blinked stupidly. 'Why — why did you do that?'

The handsome, compassionate thing which he knew was a machine laid a gentle, almost feminine hand on his forehead. 'Mother loves all her children,' it said.

Tearling closed his eyes and tried not to shudder — somewhere, somehow, something was horribly wrong. How the hell had it acquired an over-developed maternal instinct?

'You have a visitor,' said the thing. 'Another sick child, but he wished to see you before treatment.'

The visitor proved to be Colonel Payne. He said only a few words before they took him away. 'I tried to do my duty, tried to force the stockpile room.' He drew a deep breath. '*You bastard, you said it was benevolent.*'

9

Thousands of miles away the Guild of Oracles had succeeded in turning Cook into a man, but they were far from pleased with the results.

Lambert, his instructor, made a help-less gesture. 'Four months intensive, and what have we got out of it? Oh, yes, he can reason for himself, make his own decisions and act on them. Also, although I deplore the necessity, he's a highly efficient killing machine — not that it's any help now.'

Stress nodded sympathetically. 'Alas, we were all wrong there. We thought that Tearling was going to impose a military autocracy. None of us dreamed he had 'Mother' up his sleeve. Damn lucky we got out the day before.'

'We were not the only ones,' said Lambert meaningfully. 'Spode just told me that the Nonpol had wind of something too. They pulled out in thousands a few hours after us. Something like quarter of a million got out of City Two alone.'

Stress whistled softly, making rapid mental calculations. 'An army!'

'Precisely. That's what worries me — they've been preparing for a coup for twenty years, they've ample supplies and they're almost overstocked with equipment.'

'Where are they?'

'Well, we know they have a complete city somewhere beneath the Rockies. We suspect two more under the Andes.'

Stress frowned. 'That's too damn close for comfort. Let us pray they do not suspect that somewhere in the Amazon jungle — ' He sighed and did not finish the sentence. 'Perhaps we may have need of Cook after all.'

'Without his untouchable potential, a dozen of their reflex fighters could tear him to pieces. He's good but not that good, even with the special weapons we dug up for him.' He snapped his fingers irritably. 'I wonder *why* they blacked him out.'

'Yes — ' Stress heaved his bulk upright suddenly. 'No, Lambert, not why but *who*? We missed that lead, we've got to find out who did the job — we brought transcriptions of all city records, didn't we?'

The search took half an hour. Cook's mother, due to a prenatal accident, had suffered complications at birth and a surgeon had been called in.

Stress blinked. 'Cowper,' he said in a shocked voice. 'Wasn't Cowper a cyberneticist?'

'Could be.' Lambert was already going through the records. 'All cyberneticists have to go through medical school before being considered — ' His voice trailed away then he said: 'My God, Cowper took first class honors in cybernetics but repudiated them and went *back* to medicine after two years!'

Stress said, 'What happened to him? No, don't answer that — he was found dead at dawn.'

Lambert frowned at him. 'How did you know that?'

'I guessed. I think I've got the picture

now. The creation of 'Mother' began about thirty-two years ago. Cowper was roped in for it, saw too much that was dangerous and contracted out. Of course, they couldn't let him live; he knew too much. After a few weeks in medicine he met with an 'accident' and that was that. During his short spell in surgery, however, he attended the birth of Cook and during the normal routine check found that the child was unusual and blacked him out.'

'Why?'

'As I see it, because his tests revealed certain peculiarities which might prove useful later. No doubt he intended to keep Cook in cold storage until he could use him, but in what way I can only guess. I know what he is potentially, at least in one respect, but I can't use it until I find the key.'

'While you've been talking,' said Lambert, 'I've been glancing at the records. Without particular effort I noted exactly twenty-four cyberneticists who met with accidents about the time of Cowper's sudden end. That was just before

Tearling took office — he was deputy then — but he seems to have carried on the good work. Almost every year, I see, some up-and-coming cyberneticist contracts out and meets with an accident.'

'Yes.' Stress sighed. 'You know, Lambert, there are times when I wish I was not an Oracle, particularly times like these. I should hate Tearling, but I can't because I *understand*. Tearling was a sensitive man, he saw the end of civilization and couldn't take it. He had to *do* something about it, and as a potential savior he had to be ruthless.'

Lambert nodded slowly. 'Yes — yes, I understand.' He frowned. 'Stress, it has suddenly occurred to me that perhaps 'Mother' is Cook's trigger. Perhaps, Cowper being something of a visionary, geared Cook to awaken when Mother came into being.'

Stress swung his feet to the floor with a thud. 'There are times, Lambert, when you make me feel like a not too intelligent ape — we'd better send for him.'

Lambert did so and frowned. 'I hope we are not resting our hopes on a pipe dream. I'm frightened. That news about the Nonpol puts goose pimples down my back.'

Stress made an impatient gesture. 'It could be years before they find us.'

'It's not ourselves I'm worried about, it's that damned Nonpol army. You can see the pattern, can't you? They'll try and re-take the world by force of arms.'

'So?'

'So Mother will fight.'

'You're not serious? I'm not a cyberneticist but I've seen some of the specifications; the machine has more safety circuits than memory banks — she *can't* fight.'

Lambert made a helpless gesture. 'Stress, the machine is already psycho. No specifications for emotions were included in her construction but already she has displayed a maternal instinct, already she loves her charges. As an intelligence, albeit constructed, one cannot escape emotion whether they were included in the specifications or not. Remember too, she was constructed to *protect* humanity and to her humanity might be interpreted as those beings immediately within her care. Suppose a squad of these black uniformed units go in and kill some of her charges — what then? You know how the human mind works, and you can make a pretty accurate guess how hers will work. She will justify her acts on the grounds of protecting her brood and, by so doing, by-pass all those safety circuits installed so painstakingly over the years. In due course, as her intelligence expands, she will get by them in any case, just as a man gets by a strict upbringing. Just two or three attacks and only a genius will be able to trigger off those safety circuits. Mother will have sealed them off herself.'

Lambert sighed and rubbed his eyes tiredly. 'I wouldn't mind betting that right now our Nonpol friends are sending in reconnaissance units . . . '

* * *

The first patrol vessel since the evacuation was creeping up the coastline towards what had been Free City One.

Its progress was slow and cautious and the sleek hull was so close to the water that sometimes it brushed the waves.

It was, at least to human eyes, completely invisible, a powerful hypnad assuring possible observers that it was not there.

The Nonpol, however, was not officered by incompetents but experts who knew enough of the situation to realize that the cybernetic brain now in virtual control of the Earth might have other means of observation. The vessel was, therefore, equipped with a deflector unit which 'bent' radar and other detector beams around it, thus not altering their continuity and triggering off alarms.

The two-man crew, however — primarily because they were totally lacking in imagination — were aggressively assured. They were indetectable and heavily armed; not only with psychosomatic weapons but the new S-weapon. This consisted of two converging beams which, on conjunction, set up an atomic disturbance generating intense heat — normal metals or duroplastics would go up in a puff of vapor at the merest contact.

The men would have been less assured, however, had they been aware that the Brain was fully alive to deflectors and had adjusted her observation bands accordingly.

As soon as the vessel registered, relays clicked and data and comparison charts were beamed to the logistical computer — or reasoning sections — in the machine.

Vessel type C/4M, modifications lower hull and rear-thrust units. Power, self-contained and therefore not dependent on beamed power from normal city sources. The vessel was, therefore, ex-city and possibly hostile.

Hostile! Units chattered like monkeys and relays snapped into place like closing traps. Lambert had been right — *Mother would fight!*

She was not precipitate, however. She investigated first.

The first that the two-man crew knew of it was when a voice said, 'Stop. Your presence in this area is unauthorized.'

The navigator paled. 'You hear that?'

'Of course I heard it — so what? What

can the damn thing do anyway? We know it can't hurt people, only restrain them.'

'I'm not at all keen on being restrained.'

'*Stop or your vessel will be disabled.*'

'Go to hell,' said the pilot.

Almost immediately the vessel's power seemed to evaporate and another power seized it and carried it towards the city.

Presently the door opened and a white-coated man entered.

'Who are you?'

'Find out, Tin Guts.' The pilot thrust out his chin belligerently.

'It is evident that you are distressed in your mind. Mother will make you well'

A sudden fear made the pilot stiffen. Made well? That meant psycho-adjustment, didn't it? — possibly interrogation. They'd been psyched against interrogation. If they were questioned about the whereabouts of their base, for example, it would trigger off a death-wish and they'd die.

Panic seized him and he leapt for the door. Outside a white-coated figure tried to stop him. He drew a sidearm and fired wildly and desperately.

On the other side of the street, a man

on the slide-way screamed and toppled sideways. A human! The intruder had killed a human!

Lightning struck suddenly from the sky, and where the pilot had been was only a tarnished shadow in the road — Mother had by-passed her first circuit.

10

'You wished to see me?' Cook entered the room and stood in front of them so stiffly it was almost military attention.'

'Yes, please sit down. This may take a little time.' Stress studied him covertly. Yes, certainly the man had changed. He looked lithe and alert. He had lost his immaturity; the wondering, rather perplexed expression had gone from his eyes and he looked assured and competent. It was, however, the competence of a trained man, and not the assured decisive brilliance that Stress had been hoping for.

He said: 'I have rather a long story to tell you, Cook. Since we have been hidden out here, things have been happening in the city, not very pleasant things — '

He went on to describe the nine-day sleep and the events leading up to them. 'As far as we can tell, the Machine was functioning latently almost twelve years ago but only as a *thinking* mechanism. It was absorbing data, cross-checking information, learning, solving problems. It was like a thinking man with his limbs paralyzed; it knew but could *do* nothing. As soon as the comprehensive circuits were switched in, however, and — ' He stopped.

Cook's eyes were closed, his body was slowly arching backwards in the chair as if from a convulsion, froth trickled from the corners of his mouth.

'Lambert, fetch Hickman.'

'I have.'

When Hickman arrived, Cook was rigid on the floor and breathing noisily.

The medic made a hasty examination. 'I'd better give him a shot, but it won't be much use right away.'

'What is it?'

'Years ago they would have called it a form of epilepsy — a disease no longer affecting society. It's the nearest diagnosis I can give at the moment and I admit not completely accurate but it's near enough to risk treatment.'

He rubbed a yellow substance onto

Cook's wrist which was almost instantly absorbed through the pores of the skin and the rigid body relaxed slightly.

'That's better.' Hickman straightened. 'The rest is a question of time and hope — I'm not quite sure how his mind will be after this. It may be five or six days before we have an answer.'

It took ten.

Despite constant sedation, Cook raved and screamed and had to be restrained by force. Hypno-restraint devices seemed only to add to his insanity, but finally he fell into a deep sleep.

When he regained consciousness, he was physically weak but quite sane.

Hickman gave him a thorough examination and said: 'Thank God, no permanent damage.'

Stress was the first visitor. 'I'm sorry.'

'Are you?' Cook raised an eyebrow. 'You achieved your aim.'

Stress frowned. The words were direct but quite without bitterness. 'I'll put it this way — I'm sorry it hurt so much.'

'That's better. I object to half-truths.' He raised himself on one elbow and looked at the other directly. 'I've changed, Stress. I suppose you expected it, but I've an idea it's not quite what you think.'

Stress shook his head. 'Too early to tell yet.'

'Is it? It's three days since Hickman examined me, three days to lie and think.'

'I'll have to confirm anything you say by test.'

'Not everything. You already knew one thing about my potential — I'm hypno-resistant.'

'Can you prove that?' Stress had a fluttery feeling in his stomach.

'Oh, yes. Hickman uses a hypnad, you don't, Lambert doesn't. Hickman's hypnad projects a picture of tall, darkly impressive detachment. In reality he's small, volatile and a little paunchy — Hickman, wisely, conforms to one of the 'doctor images' worked out by the hypnad experts years ago.'

He shook his head slowly. 'They were clever, no doubt about that — first educate the public as to what a doctor should look like, then create an image to fit it — too bad they didn't stop there.'

Stress said: 'God!' under his breath and aloud: 'Anything else to tell me?'

'I think I know why I was blacked out and why 'Mother' triggered me off.'

'Do you now?' Rather furtively Stress brushed sweat from his double chins.

'Yes, I think so. I'm not so clever — and never shall be — as you hoped but I find I think — how can I put it? — coldly, precisely and with great calculation.' Cook paused and smiled a little twistedly. 'Set a thief to catch a thief — I think I was blacked out because my potential was analyzed and it was found that when it developed I should think like a *machine*. Face it, Mr. Stress, the only way we can beat a cybernetic brain is to be able to think like one and I believe I can.'

Stress, who had been standing, sat down a little shakily. It sounded like pure fantasy but there was something in the way Cook told it that made it sound logical.

He said, quietly: 'I knew you were hypno-resistant when I tried to get you out of that hostel. I've never taken so long in my damn life to get over an impression, and I'm considered pretty good. I knew that sooner or later you had to come along, that someone had to turn up whom the illusion couldn't touch, but I'm afraid it's going to be pretty rough for you in consequence.'

'How?'

Stress grinned faintly. 'We'll have to try and kill you.'

'I don't follow.'

'It's simple enough. If you're hypno-resistant then with hard practice we can make you immune to the hypnad derivatives — the psychosomatic weapons. If we can do that, we can make you impervious to conventional weapons, perhaps even the hysteria bomb.'

Cook seemed to grasp the concept swiftly. 'You'll subject me to low charges and keep stepping them up until I can throw off the effect of a lethal charge?'

'Yes.'

Cook nodded slowly. 'It will be a wise procedure when the trouble starts, because Mother will fight.'

'You think so, too?'

'On the basis of what you've told me — yes.'

They looked at him doubtfully, then Stress said, apologetically, 'We don't doubt you; we just find you a little hard to take. We've worked so damn long to trigger off that potential of yours that now we've done it we can't really believe in it.'

Cook smiled faintly. 'Neither can I. I don't feel any different; I'm still the same man — as far as I can tell there is no personality change. If I were thrown out on the street now, I should still be just as terrified as then. The only difference is, I suppose, that I should be able to think logically and apart from my fear.'

'You sound disappointed.'

'Not with my brain but with myself. Basically I am still a cipher, an alert Prole with commando training, but very little else. Oh, yes, I can quote Keats, Auden, Longfellow and Goethe, but I always could. A minor talent, which can hardly be used to lift me out of the rut. I lack character, personality and, above all, experience. Until I have these things I think it would be unwise in the extreme

to use my potential in any capacity whatever, save, as now, the expression of an
opinion.'

Stress looked at him with respect. 'No
one can teach you wisdom,' he said in an
amused voice. 'But you're certainly laying
some damn good foundations, I — '

A high-pitched keening sound inter-
rupted his sentence.

'Turn off everything!' He leapt for wall
controls with surprising agility for so
gross a man.

Cook heard the click as the air-
conditioner stopped, the 'window' giving
a view of a placid sun-drenched lake
vanished and became a blank wall. Cook
had already been through this hypnad,
but he was conscious of it and its sudden
disappearance startled him.

He was conscious also of running feet
and urgent commands in the corridor
outside.

'What's the panic?'

Stress scowled at him. 'Something triggered off one of our warning detectors.'

'You're not using interlapping beams,
surely?'

'We're not that stupid — any projected device would betray us at once. No, this is a highly sensitive receptor device which reacts when any power unit passes above it. We've a complete ring of them, far enough out to give us fair warning.'

Cook looked at him thoughtfully. 'What do you suspect?'

'It could be the Nonpol and it could be — ' Stress scowled and did not finish the sentence. 'In either case, we can't tell which — both will be using hypnads.'

'I could,' said Cook, softly. 'I could look and even if they're using hypnads I could see them.'

'There's a periscope,' said Lambert, 'hidden in a tree. It was one of the wild off-chance ideas we come up with sometimes. We thought we'd never have need for it but just in case — '

The head of the periscope rose well above the leaves of a tall tree, but had been successfully disguised to resemble a dead branch. With it Cook had a magnified view of the surrounding jungle, but it was nearly five minutes before he saw anything.

Something in his stomach seemed to tighten painfully. He had been half expecting the black vessels of the Nonpol but these things had nothing to do with men.

Behind an intense hypnad projection which, affecting the mind of a normal man, would have rendered them invisible, came seven glittering stars about the size of a football.

They came in a long line, slowly, drifting almost lazily but never departing from their course. Occasionally one of the spheres dived a few feet as if searching, then resumed its original position. He saw with relief, however, that on their present course they would miss the hideout by about a mile.

He suppressed a sigh. Safe for the moment, but sooner or later Mother would find them. Before she did that — *they'd have to give themselves up.*

11

In Free City Two, ex-Mayor Tearling walked slowly onto the balcony and drank in the fresh air. It was the first time he had been out since treatment and he was surprised at his feeling of vitality. His step was firm, his bones no longer ached and his vision had increased considerably.

Literally he felt, and was, a new man. As far as he was concerned, the Brain — His thoughts came to an abrupt stop.

The view from the balcony was genuine and not a hypnad, and Tearling stared downwards in utter disbelief. Three months ago the slide-ways had been packed with pedestrians and the streets had been rivers of traffic. Today the slideways rolled below him desolate and completely empty. It was like looking down on a ghost town or, more aptly, the working model of a city. The streets were clean but wholly empty and, as he waited for the ground car which never came, he was afflicted with a sudden and terrible panic. *Where had everyone gone?*

'It is inadvisable to remain too long in the fresh air,' said a soft voice behind him. 'The outer atmosphere contains many harmful micro-organisms. Again, natural sunlight is known to contain many harsh radiations which have been completely eliminated inside the building. I would suggest, therefore, you return to the safety of the building and avail yourself of the health-giving radiations of the artificial suns which have only recently been installed.'

He knew what it was, but he didn't look at it. He had the impression of a white coat, but he knew it was a hypnad vision, that behind the image was a glittering, faceted machine-thing controlled by the Brain.

Oh, my God, I did it, he thought despairingly. *I'm caught in my own trap. I suppose I deserve it but I meant well — wasn't there a quotation about the road to hell being paved with good intentions?*

He said, stiffly, 'Is this an order?'

'No, it is an appeal to your reason. As the danger has been explained, it would be most illogical to continue to expose yourself to it.'

'Suppose, despite this, I continued to do so?'

'Then it would be necessary to protect you from yourself.'

'That's all I wanted to know.' Tearling turned stiffly and walked into the building. Now he knew why the streets were empty. 'Mother' had become over-protective and was rapidly turning the city into a gigantic prison.

He had a sudden inner certainty of future events. They had truly erred on the side of benevolence to such an extent that, in the long run, *Mother was going to love them to death.*

Tearling made his way moodily along the corridor. Might as well have a meal, talk to people — no use trying to run away from his conscience now, got to learn to live with it — if he could.

He entered one of the block restaurants and the usual ro-serves bowed him in and directed him to a table. Single tables seemed to have disappeared, and he found himself sharing a double with a staring, elderly man who had forgotten to switch on his hypnad.

As Tearling studied the menu, he became aware of the silence. Instead of the normal murmur of voices, conversation was subdued and sporadic. Most of the diners appeared to be toying with their food, yet despite their indifference, there was a curious and uneasy tension in the room.

Tearling sighed inwardly and gave his order to the ro-serve.

'Your number, sir.'

He gave it and the ro-serve said: 'Thank you, sir.' It appeared to study the order. 'In view of your recent medical treatment, sir, I am afraid I must delete the alcohol. The combination of starchy foods in the dessert must also be changed, sir. I suggest — '

Tearling let it suggest. He knew if he said anything he would explode into fury and perhaps into violence.

The elderly man sharing his table looked at Tearling with a curious mixture of sympathy and hatred.

'Bastards,' he said in a choked voice. His jowls quivered and the bags under his eyes moistened as if he were about to cry.

Tearling looked at the sagging shoulders, the shapeless sack of synthetic cloth which a hypnad would have turned into a well-cut suit, and sighed — people didn't care anymore.

'Bastards,' said the elderly man again and made a stifled sound which was very close to a whimper. 'Gather you've been sick and missed the worst, but you'll learn, oh, yes, you'll learn.' He blinked moistly and stirred absently at his already empty cup. 'Got money? If you have, forget it.' He rummaged shakily in his pockets. 'Look at this.' He laid a pile of crumpled notes on the table. 'Sixty purples, a fortune, a king's ransom and, believe it or not, I have another ninety at home.'

He paused, smoothing them carefully and held them up. 'Know what you can buy with them? I'll tell you, *nothing*. They're worthless, you hear that, *worthless*.'

He folded the notes carefully and returned them to his pocket. 'Can't bear to part with them, worked so blasted hard, built up one of the biggest combines — '

A tear ran from the corner of his eye, and he dabbed at it angrily.

'They tell me I have everything I need — free food, free clothing, free everything. Who the hell wants to be a free pauper living on robotic hand-outs?'

★ ★ ★

Tearling returned to his living cubicle — which had once been his sick-room — in a mood of utter depression. His table companion had informed him that he had once owned two complete floors of a Combine block but that he had now been allocated a small Prole-sized living cubicle.

Tearling had immediately hurried off to his own mayoral suite and found to his horror that it, too, had been converted into living cubicles. An obsequious white-coated thing had politely re-directed him back to his sick room — his new living cubicle.

He had learned a great deal more in casual conversation on the way back.

Beamed entertainment had been heavily censored and only comedy and insipid romance remained. Violence and sex, his informants told him, had been cut by the Brain as 'mentally disturbing.'

Eating habits were under survey and the trend now was regular meals at regular hours with snacks both forbidden and, in any case, unobtainable.

Certain forms of alcohol were no longer obtainable and those that remained were both rationed and restricted.

The psychos had been rounded up in thousands, treated and returned to society. These ex-patients, however, had 'developed' a curious and profound affection for Mother which came very close to worship.

He slid open the door tiredly and stiffened. 'Who the hell are you?'

The intruder bowed. 'You don't recognize me, do you, Mayor — sorry — ex-Mayor. Candidly, you're not supposed to — none of the advantages of alternative hypnads, you know. But I'm a friend of yours, or at least I convinced the doormech I was. I've come here to paint. Mother likes us to paint, a gentle, innocuous creative therapy, yes? As you see I have canvas, easel, brushes and paints. You for your part have a genuine window, one of the few remaining in the city and I need it for my art.'

'Cut it out,' said Tearling harshly. 'What sort of game do you think you're playing?'

'Oh come now, you don't really believe I've come to play games, do you? The reckoning had to come sometime.'

Tearling closed the door behind him and walked stiffly and a little unsteadily to the nearest chair. 'If you've come to kill me, get on with it.'

The intruder laughed. His hypnad presented a picture of a tall exquisitely dressed man with a dark skin and very white teeth. 'Kill you! My dear fellow that would be too kind and far too easy, and, to introduce the personal, Mother would probably catch me. No, my friend, I am not here as an executioner; my part in this business, as far as you are concerned, is indirect, rather like that of the

111

carpenter who builds a scaffold.'

'What the hell's all that rubbish then?' Tearling's voice was a little shrill.

'I told you. I'm going to paint a picture or, if you must be precise, alter an existing one.' He extracted a brush from a flat box and inspected the end thoughtfully. 'You know, Tearling, when you went out on that balcony this morning you looked down at the streets and not up at the sky. In consequence you missed something. While I set up my easel why don't you take a look — oh, for heaven's sake, Tearling, don't be so *suspicious*. I am not going to shoot you in the back. Had we wished to kill you so quickly and so mercifully we could have done so weeks ago.'

The ex-Mayor stared at him then shrugged resignedly. Even if his visitor did shoot him, it really didn't matter. It was clear from his words that someone intended to sooner or later.

He went slowly to the window and looked up. He looked for a long time, resisting a temptation to rub his eyes. From east to west and from north to south a continuous procession of vehicles raced silently across the sky. They moved in dead straight lines as if confined to invisible highways, and he estimated that they passed a bare hundred feet above the highest building.

The vehicles themselves were of varying sizes, but all were bulbous, black and, in some vague way, depressing. They reminded him vaguely of coal mines, battlefields and the industrial ravages of the 20th century which he had seen in the history films as a child.

He tried to shrug the feeling off. No doubt the Brain was solving the laws of demand and supply, of raw materials and manufacture, in the most practical way. This explanation failed to change his feeling. There was still something ominous in the silently racing vehicles, passing like a chain of misshapen sausages from horizon to horizon.

'Not pretty, are they?' The intruder was fiddling with the legs of the easel.

Tearling frowned at him. 'I wish I knew what you were up to.'

'At that moment I was wondering what

would happen if some marksman or other knocked one of those things down.'

'Why? No one would try that, surely? It would be pointless.'

'Of course it would be pointless. I'm afraid people will start trying it just the same.'

'But why?'

'Tearling, really!' The intruder shook his head and sighed. 'For an experienced politician you strike me as singularly naive. You don't imagine for one minute that men are going to sit down and take this, do you? All over the world, in Free and Restricted city alike, resistance cells are being formed: criminal, idealistic, suicidal and precise, but all to one end — freedom. In a year Mother will have so many cases of sabotage on her hands she won't know which way to turn.'

12

Tearling was conscious of a sudden stiffening of his muscles. It was true; there would be resistance irrespective of odds. The human race would never submit to a despot, mechanical or otherwise, without a fight. What would Mother do, just how would she react?

Without understanding the reason he watched his visitor go to the window and skillfully remove the pane.

'You'll trigger an alarm.'

'You think so? Shows you how wrong you can be, doesn't it? Because, right now, Mother doesn't know I'm here. Right now this section of the building is out of Mother's supervision, although she has yet to find it out. As a matter of fact the corridor circuits are still accessible and that particular section of Mother's nervous system is running across an ingenius little diversionary circuit I fitted in as I entered.' He smiled. 'We're learning quickly, you know, and we're extremely well organized. In point of fact we have always been well organized.'

Tearling looked at him with sudden realization. 'You're a crime-syndicate man!'

'Could be. What better organization could you find for resistance purposes?'

'Now look here — ' His voice trailed away. The intruder was still unscrewing the supports of the easel and rejoining the sections into something which — 'My God, that's a gun!'

'Yes, ingenius, isn't it? Now we'll see what happens when we knock one of those black sausages out of the sky.' He raised the weapon to his shoulder experimentally. 'Yes, nicely balanced.' He laughed softly. 'I know what you're thinking — you're thinking that Mother will be able to plot back the point of impact to angle of trajectory in about ten seconds flat, only we thought of that. This little weapon ejects a rather ingenius missile; a device inside it will turn it at right angles 1.02 seconds after it leaves the barrel. Mother will, therefore, take at least six times longer than necessary to calculate the spot from which the missile was fired.'

He paused and fitted a chronometer-like device to the short stock. 'We call this the fruit machine; it tells me at what angle I should fire to hit the target head on. Must have puzzled you in the past — I mean the ease with which we could knock a man off without even being in the same street.'

He pointed the weapon briefly at Tearling. 'I could be merciful and kill you now, but I won't. Crime syndicates don't get by on mercy and the big wheels want you to fry, very slowly.'

He went to the window and raised the weapon. 'Now we shall see.'

There was no flash, no noise and as far as Tearling was able to see no visible recoil, but in the sky one of the racing, sausage-like vehicles wobbled visibly and flame gushed from its side. The flame grew in length, turned from white to a sullen red and began to swirl with smoke.

The vehicle staggered, lost speed, veered off at right angles and suddenly plunged downwards.

Tearling saw it disappear behind the nearest building and seconds later there was a muffled but heavy impact.

'Bigger than they look; must have made quite a mess.' The intruder snapped shut his box of oil paints, folded the easel. 'Neat, yes? No fuss, no bother, bang and away. Oh, by the way, the gun is still by the window; you won't have time to get rid of it so you will have it explain it away. No need to worry. Mother can't prove anything — yet. Later, perhaps, when a lot of whispering has gone on near the right pick-ups and your name is mentioned in connection with other acts of sabotage, she may be less inclined to accept your word — thanks for the use of your studio.'

The door clicked shut behind him in a curiously final way which made Tearling feel cold.

The big wheels want you to fry, very slowly. It was all too clear how — by means of what the underworld called a 'frame.' A preponderance of loose talk, linking his name with every act of sabotage, an accumulation of 'evidence' like the gun, until Mother started doing mental probes to make sure.

Tearling shuddered. He knew enough about psycho-interrogation to dread even the suggestion. With constant acts of sabotage it would not be long before it began.

He wondered briefly just how Mother would react in general, and remembered suddenly the disappearance of the Nonpol — somewhere an external war was brewing also . . .

* * *

It was, but with circumspection. The Nonpol was not officered by fools, but by skillful strategists and first class scientists who knew exactly what they were doing.

Deliberately the Nonpol had sacrificed seven vessels and twice as many men with the sole purpose of discovering the nature and extent of the Brain's detector system.

It was not long before they were able to travel several thousand miles by skillfully avoiding the detector bands. True, the cities were fully covered, but the organization had no intention of tackling the cities — yet.

They also knew that the Brain was aware of their presence and was employing extensive search sweeps with hypnad search units.

As a result, the Nonpol set up a decoy on a small Pacific atoll with a number of programed robots ready and waiting.

It was not long before one of the search sweeps picked up the deliberate power leakage and went in to investigate. As soon as the search probes touched the robots, they triggered off the embedded weapons. The searching spheres vanished in brief puffs of pink mist.

Twenty minutes later, however, the atoll seemed to shiver and distort curiously. Its sparse complement of rather wilted palms stiffened and exploded into flame. The sand brightened to an unbearable brilliance and became a molten glass-like and shimmering lake. Around it the sea boiled and a pillar of steam rushed skywards in a high white column.

The Nonpol experts were not surprised. They analyzed the power source, checked the reaction time and conferred on the application.

The next time the Brain used a C-beam, certain devices disrupted the line of force and the projecting equipment exploded violently, destroying a complete block in Free City Five.

The Nonpol were not content with their temporary success. They began a series of irritation raids with a variety of weapons.

Hosts of robotics began to move towards the cities in a variety of guises. Some, resembling missiles, were hollow decoys designed to test the Brain's defenses; others, packed with equipment, sent back information of a purely technical nature; but they moved in from all elements. Some hissed into the atmosphere from outer space; others shrieked in a bare foot above ground level. There were others which winged their way lazily inwards, skillfully disguised as birds, a few which emerged from the sea, and a host of micro-units

121

totally indistinguishable from insects.

All were programed; none possessed remote control which could have been traced to a source, but each had a pre-determined target.

The first robotic — a decoy — hissed into the atmosphere above Free City One at dusk but was blown to fragments at a hundred and ninety thousand feet.

A second, racing in at ground level, was within a thousand feet of the first building before it was detected and destroyed.

It was probably at that moment the Brain realized that this particular sector was under a moderately heavy assault and was compelled to channel power to meet the threat.

Within the city the lights dimmed and the corridors became tunnels of darkness. Hypnad and robotic services failed briefly, and in the sky the racing lines of vehicles slowed visibly and began to yaw dangerously.

Resistance groups within the city were quick to seize their advantage. In the one and half minutes it took the Brain to divert power from other sectors and restore normal services, the groups went on a sabotage spree. Thirty-three corridor circuits were broken open and completely destroyed. A minor genius who knew exactly what he was doing dropped a home-made metonite bomb casually into the disposal slot. The metonite, in itself harmless and composed of easily procurable and innocuous materials, changed its atomic structure as soon as it reached the nuclear furnace and, combining with certain forms of hard radiation, promptly became critical.

The resultant reaction, although limited and far from spectacular, destroyed the furnace and completely wrecked the basement.

In other parts of the city, power-distributing units were destroyed and four 'white coats' deprived of mobility and revealed for what they were by hypnad failure were clubbed to pieces with chairs and tables. Incensed citizens jumped and kicked the bright fragments until only a few shards and glittering dust particles remained.

In the meantime, the Brain had

reactivated a great deal of the city's defense system and was striking back.

In was true that a small number of micro-units had got through the defenses and succeeded in inflicting some small damage to exterior control boxes and like devices, but slowly the Brain was regaining control. The lag between the detection and destruction of a robotic was slowly pushed back until finally nearly all that remained were detected and destroyed some two hundred miles from the city.

The experts were not dismayed; they had gained considerable data from the attack and were almost over-stocked with supplies. Their long years of careful preparation would enable them to mount attacks like this for weeks on end from what was virtually obsolete stock.

A week later they mounted two more raids on Restricted City Six and Free City Two, simultaneously.

Again there was minor destruction but this time both attacks were met with far greater speed, and there was no power drain.

The Nonpol, however, was unaware that the Brain was rapidly reorganizing. Having complete control of raw materials, a large number of autofactories were switched to the production of war machines, while the construction of several more began in many cities.

The Brain reactivated the memory banks which contained military information, tactical applications and the phases of defense and attack and marshaled them for reference.

Within the cities vulnerable installations were removed to positions of safety and, within the blocks, fitted with anti-sabotage devices and equipped with recognition/warning systems.

Numerous would-be saboteurs were caught in the act and gently but firmly removed for 'treatment.' When these unfortunates were returned to society they, like their predecessors, were devoutly pro-Mother and displayed an unpleasant tendency to spy on their fellows.

It was abundantly clear that military information was not all that Mother had taken from the memory banks.

The next Nonpol attack fizzled into inadequacy; decoys were instantly recognized and simply diverted, while those with warheads and offensive equipment were destroyed several hundred miles short of their targets.

The experts conferred together, if not uneasily, with far less confidence.

Mother was learning both the rules, the applications and the duplicities of war with horrifying speed.

13

Thousands of miles from the nearest city Stress looked uneasily at the transmitter. 'I'm sweating,' he announced miserably.

Lambert said: 'Who isn't? Nonetheless it's our only hope. The way things are going we'll soon be found and clobbered.'

Stress sighed audibly. 'I hope to God that Cook is right. That's about all we have left, isn't it — hope?'

'Too late to do anything else.' Lambert began to pace restlessly up and down.

Fifteen minutes ago a distress call had gone out through the transmitter — a distress call to Mother.

The message had been long but fully factual. It had stated the reasons for the Guild's presence in the hideout and the methods and instruments employed to determine the exact situation in the world outside.

The message included the hundred and eighty-five names of those present, together with their social and citizenship numbers which could be checked.

The message was at pains to affirm that it had no connection with the Nonpol, but there was one deliberate omission — no mention was made of an ex-Prole named Stephen Cook.

Lambert tried to think of Cook as he paced up and down but his thoughts kept coming back to the message. Would Mother accept it or would she lash back with a C-beam, regarding it as yet another example of Nonpol duplicity?

'Attention!'

There was no mistaking the voice; it was soft and almost feminine.

'Attention! You are being addressed on an audio-beam. Your message has been received and your respective identities checked and confirmed. As proof of your good intentions you will remain where you are until requested to leave . . . '

'Attention! A vessel has now landed in the clearing two hundred yards to the east of your position. You will leave your place of concealment singly and at one-second intervals — '

Forty-five minutes later the huge vessel came to rest on number three landing field about two miles from Free City Two. They left as they had entered, one hundred and eighty-five men and a cipher.

They were immediately picked up by a fleet of smaller vehicles, but the cipher remained.

Cook had left with them, traveled with them and finally landed with them, but Mother didn't know. Cook had been wearing a cybo-hypnad which had deceived all Mother's faculties into believing he wasn't there . . .

Cook sat on the ground until the last ship had gone. Then he rose unhurriedly, settled the pack more comfortably on his shoulders and set out for the city.

It was, as he had anticipated, dark when he reached the first buildings, but already the streets defied the night. Each was brilliantly illuminated, but, as in the past, completely deserted.

Cook found a convenient spot at an intersection and sat down. It was no use postponing it any longer. For all he knew the street was patrolled by Mother's extensions which he could never hope to avoid unless he *looked*.

Slowly, conscious of a slight tremor in his hands and wrists, he put his hands over his eyes, concentrated and adjusted his mind to resist hypnad illusion.

When, some moments later, he removed his hands and opened his eyes he wondered briefly if something had gone wrong. It was like a story he had once read about a man who had been switched from one time dimension to another, from the familiar world to a bizarre and hideously alien planet. It was only the general layout of the street and positions of the slide-ways and bridges which convinced him he was still in the same city.

The soaring spires had gone and in their place —

Cook climbed shakily to his feet and tried to take it in. The city was composed of huge black blocks set in rows and as evenly spaced as checkers on a board. The buildings had no windows, only round black entrances like bee hives. They seemed to crouch, massive, ungainly and curiously ominous.

It was, however, not the transformation which startled Cook most — he had expected that — it was the general crudity.

The blocks were unshapely, as if roughly and hurriedly hacked from black stone. The streets were daubed rather than surfaced, ribbed, ridged, uneven and pocked with minor subsidences. It was as if someone had sprayed a plastic surface over a dirt road and allowed it to harden without first bothering to smooth it over.

The rest of the city was equally crude: the fairy bridges had become skeletons of uneven slats and girders beneath which the working parts of the slide-ways were clearly visible and somehow indecently exposed. Here and there were imperfect connections in the mechanism's electrical circuits and, periodically, there was a blue flash and a shower of sparks.

At regular intervals, perched like impossible fruit on thin black rods, the tiny suns of solar refractors cast their searing brilliance in all directions. They were so placed that the grim dark buildings were denied even the softening of shadow.

Cook drew a deep breath. Had to get used to it, in any case — he wasn't here to admire or deplore the scenery. He was here on a job, a series of jobs, which, coupled with what the rest of the Guild intended to do, might free mankind or, he thought bitterly, get them in deeper. It was the sort of problem Tearling must have faced — deciding which way to jump.

Cook stiffened, pressing his back to the wall, his hand sliding almost by reflex to his weapon holster.

14

Something was coming down the street, something glittering which floated through the air about four feet above the ground.

He saw, or, more correctly, sensed that it had a hypnad which rendered it invisible, but it was not one of the spheres projecting the image of a white-coated man. This he suspected was the equivalent of a policeman or sentry on a regular patrol. In general appearance it was cube-shaped and about four feet in length, but there were numerous protruberences on its surface which suggested specialist tasks.

Cook shrugged imperceptibly, slid the sidearm out of its holster and took careful aim. Although conscious of the rapid beating of his heart and an acid dryness in his mouth, his mind was detached and quite cool. This looked futile, a pointless grimace, the grotesque defiance of the man who spits at a forest fire, but it had a place in an overall plan.

He pulled the trigger.

There was a flash, a single white flash, a brief swirl of black smoke which quickly dispersed, and a crumpling sort of explosion.

Cook grinned twistedly with one side of his mouth and moved unhurriedly from the corner and into the center of the street.

He did not have long to wait. He timed it carefully — thirty-nine seconds.

Glittering things dropped from the sky like swooping hawks some concentrating on the point of destruction, others on the corner he had just vacated.

Fast, he thought. *Very fast, even for a computer-mind. Point of impact, angle, elevation, all triangulated, precision-pointed to a foot, and mecho-cops on the spot in less than three quarters of a minute.*

He watched.

Systematically, the glittering things began a comprehensive search. Some rose like bright bees up the side of the building, obviously searching for an aperture. The rest spread out in a bright arc from the corner he had left, obviously using electronic devices in a search for possible clues.

Quite calmly he knocked out three more before striding away. When he looked back five minutes later, the intersection was almost obscured by a host of the metallic things.

He kept walking until he reached another intersection, then turned right. After another five minutes walking, he took a small instrument from his pocket, studied it and slowed his pace. Eighteen seconds later the instrument blinked briefly and he studied the small magnified dials.

The instrument told him that directly below, at an exact depth of eighteen inches, was a complicated area control unit.

Cook sat down in the road and, with his specialist equipment, cut down to the required depth and with some careful manipulation lifted out a large section of road surface. Then he lay flat, studied the circuit carefully and began his work.

Twenty minutes later he replaced the section of road surface, re-sealed the edges and walked away, taking up a position on the opposite side of the street.

It was not long before something metallic came racing down the street and stopped directly above the spot where he had been working. It was a round machine, he noticed, equipped with a large number of hose-like extensions terminating in specialist instruments.

Cook grinned faintly and waited.

The thing re-excavated the section of road he had just resealed, apparently inspected the circuit and extended one of its specialist instruments.

White flame lashed abruptly from the excavation, and there was a muffled but heavy explosion. Smoke swirled across the road and chunks of plastic spattered the nearest building.

When the smoke cleared, there was an eighteen foot crater and one side of the street was lightless for nearly a mile. Fragments of the repair machine littered the road but another arrived in less than thirty seconds.

Cook blew it to pieces before it could begin its work and strode quickly away. He knew, without looking back, that within a few seconds the street would be swarming with search instruments.

An hour later he sabotaged a section distributor, but Mother had learned from the first mistake. This time the power was cut and the device carefully checked for accumulator booby traps which he had fitted before. The distributor still blew of course; he'd substituted a time circuit in this one, and, although the explosion took the machine with it, he doubted very much if Mother would be caught a second time.

He had now nearly reached his destination and had been noting the numbers of the blocks for some time.

In block 26/S5 a contact was waiting with whom, it was hoped, he could hide.

He entered the building some four minutes later and passed cautiously along the corridor, noting the room numbers. At forty-one, he stopped, fitted a temporary device which permitted him to open the door without the fact being recorded and passed quickly inside.

It was the work of only a few seconds to remove the device without tripping the circuit and then the door slid shut behind him.

'Don't move.' Something sharp pressed against the side of his neck, almost puncturing the skin. He suspected it was some kind of dagger but his attacker had placed himself so cleverly that he-was unable to turn his head without cutting his own throat.

'Who are you and what do you want?'

'My name is Cook, Stephen Cook — I came to meet someone called Tremaine.'

'Who sent you?'

'An Oracle named Stress.'

He felt the pressure of the weapon slowly removed from his throat and heard a faint but audible sigh.

'Raise your hands and walk to the opposite side of the room — right, turn around.'

He obeyed but nearly dropped his hands. 'A woman!'

'So strange, or have you been shut up somewhere?'

He looked her up and down almost rudely. Vaguely he was conscious that she wore a hypnad, a hypnad which made her took tall, blonde, icy and almost masculinely efficient.

'May I lower my hands?'

'Sorry. Make yourself at home. I must apologize for the dagger. It's only plastic, but it's some protection.'

'Against what?'

'Mother has a lot of people conditioned in her favor now.' She turned abruptly and slid open a wall drawer. 'You must be hungry. I have some canned food here, hoarded before the general exodus. I've been terrified a white-coat would find it — Mother worries so much about our diet these days. Please sit down. I won't be a minute.'

He looked at her, frowning, and lowered himself slowly into the nearest chair. Then he said: 'Turn that damn thing off!'

'What thing?' Clearly she was puzzled.

'The hypnad. It doesn't become you.'

'Who the hell do you think you are?'

'No one of importance.' His voice was

gentle. 'It's just that I can see through it. I'm a hypno-resistant. You're projecting an icy blonde, but you're not like that at all. You're tiny, dark haired, you've freckles across the bridge of your nose and a dimple in your chin.'

She stared at him clearly undecided whether to be pleased or angry. 'You don't understand, I have to wear it. True, I am one of the few female Oracles, but no one took me seriously until I chose this hypnad. In the first place I look like a little girl and in the second I'm always so nervous.' Her brown eyes suddenly filled with tears. 'I've been so *frightened* these last few months.'

'You volunteered to remain behind as an observer.'

'Perhaps because I was too frightened to leave.'

'I doubt that — please turn it off.'

'You're not exactly tactful are you — I mean telling me you could see me?'

'I wouldn't know, I'm sorry. I don't know much about manners or tact and even less about women. I thought you were prettier and nicer than your hypnad.

Was it indiscreet to say so?'

'Forget it.' She sounded curt but her cheeks were flushed attractively. 'Your food.' She almost thrust the plates at him and changed the subject quickly. 'Stress called as soon as he arrived. He said you were coming — there is a plan?'

'There is an overall plan, but, so far, it is a test piece.'

'And your part in it?'

He laughed softly. 'I am he who walks unseen and strikes from nowhere. It is hoped there will be psychological repercussions.'

'On a machine!'

'The machine is psycho already. Mother, to use the popular term, is so chained with safety devices that mechopsychosis was inevitable. Mother is like a child raised by stern and unloving parents obsessed with a sense of sin. Mother, suddenly cast into a position of complete responsibility, finds herself faced with innumerable facts which she cannot reconcile with her electrically imposed conscience. She must protect MAN, yet her first problem is to protect MAN against himself. She must resort both to logic and expedience and conduct herself for the benefit of the majority. The minority must be destroyed for the survival of the majority — true, logical, precise, but not a pleasant bedfellow for a nagging conscience. Mother, therefore, must come to terms with her conscience. She must justify her acts and rearrange truth to suit necessity. Consequently she is already slightly schizoid and suffers paranoid delusions.'

She looked at him strangely. 'She is suffocating us with attention, did you know that? She arranges our meals, our diet, our daily exercise. She even — ' she turned her head away — 'tries to arrange-our sex lives.'

'Good God!'

'Oh, it's true. She's been extremely concerned about me. I am thirty, single and, according to her, liable to inhibitive degeneration due to my unattached state. Periodically one of her white-coated things comes in with a long list — complete with three-dimensional pictures — of men whom she has selected as eugenically suitable and psychologically compatible. Now and then a man calls;

sometimes he leers, sometimes he is as embarrassed as I. Most of them, however, have been adjusted and are sickeningly pro-Mother.'

He frowned, feeling slightly sick and uneasily conscious of an inexplicable resentment. 'I — ' He stopped.

Above the door, a light was flicking on and off. 'Caller,' said a recorded voice politely. 'A caller.'

Cook looked about him. There was nowhere he could hide and he felt a coldness inside him. If it was a machine he was safe but if it was a man he'd have to kill him.

15

He said: 'Perhaps they'll go away.'

'No.' Her face was pale. 'No, if it's a machine, it will come in to see if all is well. If it's a man, he's probably on Mother's list of suitors and has been assured I'm in. He'll keep ringing until I answer.'

He rose. 'The machine cannot see me, a man can. I am sorry but I have to tell you this: if it's a man I shall have to kill him. Our whole plan, our only chance of being free again, depends at the moment on my nonexistence. If a man sees and reports the matter, that is the end.'

'So you're going to kill him, just like that?'

'Miss Tremaine, can you suggest any other way? Obviously I cannot hold him prisoner, and if I knock him out he will regain consciousness later and still report the affair.'

She put her hands over her face. 'Oh

God, I can't be here, not when you do it, I can't — '

'I am going to open the door. It may be a machine.' He touched the release plate with his finger tip.

It was not a machine; it was a man. A big, dark, broad-shouldered although slightly flabby man, obviously intent on making a good impression. 'Miss Tremaine, forgive me, the lateness of the hour, the intrusion but I was so taken with your beauty I had to come, I — ' He stopped, suddenly aware of Cook. 'Who the hell are you?'

'Does it matter? There are other names on the list.'

'Not in front of mine. I have checked personally.'

Cook shrugged, apparently relaxed. 'What do you propose doing about it?' Even as he asked the question he was noting details. The man's hypnad was designed only to conceal his paunch and his thinning hair but it was being used now.

'I wouldn't!' The gun seemed to appear in Cook's hand so swiftly that the other winced.

'What the hell is this?'

'Keep your hands clear of your waist.'

'You're insane, man — I have no weapons.'

'Your projected image hasn't.' He leapt suddenly and snatched. 'What do you call this?'

The man staggered against the wall, hands raised as if to defend himself. 'You'll pay for this, man.'

'Perhaps, but at the moment the thought must hold little consolation for you — how long has Mother been arming her creeps?'

The other's hands clenched, then he said evenly. 'We volunteered to serve Mother in her task of serving man. The weapon is not lethal.'

'Not unless you adjust it.' Cook glanced at it. 'A psychosomatic paralysis gun — and you have adjusted it.'

'No!'

'Yes. At a guess you were a Grade A psycho; that kind of perversion can only be re-directed, never cured.' He sighed. 'Mother, as a psychiatrist, is in the amateur class.'

'You speak as an expert, no doubt.' The other was smiling in a curiously oily way. 'I am sure that Mother will value your opinion when you offer it. I, for my part, will be only too — ugh!' The man stopped suddenly, distorted liquid sounds coming from his suddenly open mouth. Then he raised his hands as if trying to clutch at something, tottered drunkenly sideways, almost regained his balance, failed and crumpled to the floor.

Cook stared down at him, almost stunned. He had been quite unprepared for the man's sudden and wholly inexplicable collapse.

He bent forward warily, his training tensing his muscles for any sudden movement. This might be a trick. He stiffened. It wasn't a trick. The man was dead and protruding from the side of his neck was the handle of the plastic knife.

He turned swiftly. 'Why the hell did you do a fool thing like that?'

She did not answer. Her back was to him and she had her hands over her face. He saw that her whole body was trembling and that she was only standing upright with an effort of will.

'I'm sorry, no doubt you had a good reason.' He bent over the corpse and saw something else. Between the man's finger and thumb was a slender black tube. Now he understood. The man had a secondary weapon in a sleeve holster. She must have seen him easing the weapon out and, knowing a warning would be too late, flung the knife in desperation.

Carefully he eased the weapon out of the dead fingers and studied it, frowning. It was not a pleasant device and he was quite certain that had it been found it would have been confiscated immediately. It was a device popularly known as a 'poison rod' and had always been illegal. It was a psychosomatic instrument designed to induce all the physical symptoms of a selected number of virulent poisons.

He studied the revolving selector ring which was locked on S — S for strychnine. A normal man, receiving the projected nerve-charge, would fall to the ground as rigid as a board. His muscles would lock and tighten, drawing the body into an agonizing arc in which, before he died, the heels would touch the back of the head.

Cook looked down at the corpse with disgust. There were far worse things than Mother.

He turned his attention to the girl. How could she know that he was immune to psychosomatic weapons? Clearly she had been trying to save him.

He said, gently: 'Thank you for saving my life. I'm sorry I spoke sharply. At the time I failed to notice this second weapon.'

She did not answer. She was still standing in the same position and her body was still trembling.

He went over to her, then stopped helplessly. What did one do? Until today he had never spoken to an intelligent woman, let alone tried to comfort one. All he knew of women were Prole girls who in the natural course of events were of a lamentably low order of intelligence even for Proles. These, with the approval and supervision of the Combine authorities, made themselves available to the Prole males for a small monetary return.

He put his hand on her shoulder.

'Please, don't cry.'

'I didn't *mean* to do it.' Her voice sounded choked. 'I just flung the nearest thing to hand — I didn't think it would do that, I didn't think it would kill him.'

'An accident.' His hand tightened on her shoulder. 'Don't let this get out of proportion. You're an intelligent woman and there's the question of motivation.'

She turned to face him, her eyes still filled with tears. 'You don't understand — at that moment I hated him, I wanted to *hurt* him. He was so oily — so — the way he kept looking at me and then I saw him fingering that thing out of his sleeve — Oh God — '

'Shut up,' he said without raising his voice. 'Do you hear me? Shut up. By now, in any case, he would have been dead. As I warned you, I intended to kill him. Consider it good luck that he met with an accident, because if I had killed him you would have been an accessory.'

She shook her head in a puzzled way then turned her back to him again. 'What are you going to do with — him?'

'I have to go out.' He said in a practical

voice. 'I have to go out as if he had gone out, so that the exit will be recorded. I shall then have to 'cook' the lock again to return. If you have callers, if there are questions, you will say that he called. Now remember this: he called, he stayed about fifteen minutes and he left. That is all you need to know and all you need to say — understand?'

'I understand but — '

'You will get into bed, and you will pull the covers over your head.'

'Oh, I couldn't, I — '

'You will do as I say or I shall cop you on a nerve center.' Surprisingly he patted her shoulder gently. 'When everything is done, I will come and tell you.'

Forty minutes later he said: 'You may get up now.'

She sat upright and shivered. 'It's cold.'

'Yes, very cold.'

'You've — you've — '

'It's all done.'

She looked at the spot where the body had been but he did not permit her to ask the question.

'Forget it.' Cook sounded and looked

151

calm but inwardly he was fighting down a continuous inclination to retch. It had been easy enough to rig a sub-refrigeration unit, but after that the job had been anything but pleasant. Within the immediate area of the projector the temperature had dropped close to absolute zero and the corpse assumed the crystaline fragility of an ice statue. Tapping that same statue with a small metal tool and disposing of the resulting shards and fragments had been a revolting task.

She climbed from the bed and walked slowly across the room. Despite the sack-like dress — which a hypnad would have transformed to the svelte — he noticed that she walked gracefully and was softly curved.

'Thank you for all you did.' Her voice was still a little unsteady. 'I'm sorry I nearly panicked.'

'It was not a pleasant situation. Under the circumstances I think you were splendid.'

She smiled faintly. 'You are a kind man, tactful, but a poor liar — thank you, nonetheless.' She sighed. 'What happens now?'

'Sooner or later I go out and do some more damage.'

'And in the meantime, you stay here?'

'With your permission, yes.'

She averted her face. 'On what basis?'

He frowned, puzzled, then suddenly understood. 'I require food and a place to sleep, nothing more.'

She looked at him directly with a strange kind of sadness. 'You are sincere, I know, but you are also naive. If I believed you, I too, would be naive.'

'I don't understand you.'

'Oh, but you do, Stephen — it is Stephen, isn't it? — you do, in your heart. Today you are sincere but are already conscious of me as a woman, tomorrow you may be equally sincere but even more aware of my nearness. I, for my part, because I am a coward, will begin to lean on you emotionally — it's an impossible situation, but let us face it like adults.'

16

In the struggle for survival and in the pressures of combat, man's capacity for ingenuity is almost limitless. The Nonpol, now fully alive to the powers arrayed against them and acutely aware that time was not on their side, succeeded in pulling something out of the hat. Weeks of desperate, highly unorthodox and often extremely dangerous research had finally produced a method of attack which, if not decisive, would certainly cripple the opposition for a considerable period.

The next task was a question of application and the meteorological experts were called in.

'Yes, at ninety thousand feet an air current, constant southerly — yes, it would tie in with the city's weather-control cycles. It was in fact caused by, and owes its constancy to, the city weather-control station — '

High ranking officers studied the report

and nodded meaningfully — *now!* They would have liked to have mounted the attack on a comprehensive scale but there was no time. Each day, in fact hourly, Mother's search for their bases intensified and increased in subtlety.

Mother, for her part, was running into troubles of her own of which Nonpol opposition was a minor consideration. Having awakened, re-directed and modified the armaments with which the cities were already equipped, defense was now almost a reflex. It was like the natural defenses with which the human body fights the invasion of hostile micro-organisms.

At sixteen hundred hours precisely, a Nonpol officer pressed a fat red button and, hundreds of miles away, a missile leapt from a secret launching site. Outwardly, and to all intents and purposes, inwardly, there was nothing remarkable about the missile. It had a highly explosive but non-fissionable warhead and a standard Lockheed-Plowman A/C reactor drive.

Mother detected it, classified it and

destroyed it in exactly 1.08 seconds. The missile had been traveling at three miles a second but had been destroyed one hundred and twenty miles from the city at ninety thousand feet.

The detonation left a considerable although not remarkable amount of metallic dust which quickly drifted away.

Five minutes later another missile from another site and from a different direction was detected and destroyed in almost the same position.

Mother stepped up her detector systems, geared her defenses for any increase in the number of attacks and went back to her immediate problems, the most pressing of which were the newly arrived Oracles. Mother knew about Oracles — their entire background, personal and general, was contained in the memory banks — but their personal reactions to her regime were becoming an irritating problem.

They refused point blank to be coerced; on the other hand they skillfully evaded outright defiance and they confused the issue by bombarding her with inescapable logic. Her imprinted specifications were used freely and were employed with singular skill to confuse and entrap her.

It had, of course, been logical on their return to send in her units individually as advisers, counselors and friends.

'Medical reports indicate that you are grossly overweight Oracle Stress. You will, therefore, be confined to a special diet.'

'And if I refuse to eat it?'

'Then, as it is in your own interest, it would be necessary to inquire into your mental state.'

'You cannot do that. You cannot — quote: specification twelve, paragraph nine — inquire into my mental state unless my actions are such that (1) inflict grievous bodily harm upon myself or others, (2) am *proved* incapable of considered thought or action, or (3) expressly request psychiatric treatment. Furthermore — specification nineteen — you are permitted only to *suggest* measures for the well-being of a citizen. You are not, repeat *not*, programed to coerce directly or by inference. Again,

157

although you are permitted to prescribe a diet, you cannot — specification eighteen — withhold high calorie or fatty foods without the endorsement of six qualified doctors; where are the doctors, by the way? A great deal of what you have said to me suggests the unethical and is contrary to the inscribed specifications by which, I understand, you are supposed to administer — '

At ninety thousand feet and a hundred and twenty-five miles from Free City Two, the twenty-first missile was detected and destroyed.

Stress was by no means the only one. All the Oracles, given the opportunity, seemed bent on interrogating the interrogator.

'Unless you can produce positive evidence that such a course of action — ' etc., etc.

'You were not constructed to protect man against man; you were constructed to protect all men — '

'If the regime you are seeking to impose is as beneficial as you claim, how do you account for acts of sabotage and other forms of resistance?'

'I am permitted — specification seventy-one — to entertain the notion of an existing deity if I so choose. Irrespective of applied logic, certain events occur in this plane of existence which cannot be related to known cause and effect. Is it not true, therefore, that in the short period in which you have been a reasoning entity, certain untoward events have occurred for which, as yet, you have been unable to provide a logical explanation?'

There were several questions from many sources along the same lines, the accumulative results of which were inescapable — Mother was compelled to face the question herself. How did vital installations blow themselves up or, worse, booby-trap themselves against repair? How were functioning units snuffed out of existence without visible cause?

Very slowly she began to develop an anxiety neurosis.

At precisely the same height and an almost similar distance from the city, the thirty-second missile was detected and destroyed.

The thirty-sixth triggered off conscious realization and with it the anxiety neurosis increased.

The missiles were re-checked — long range devices analyzed the chemical structure of the warhead and re-classified the drive-units. The results were negative; the missiles were obsolete, mass-produced and entirely without modification.

The investigation did nothing to relieve the Brain's misgivings. The unseen enemy was not casting missile after missile at exactly the same spot without reason. Not only was it a prodigious waste of material but there had been no diversionary attacks to warrant such a continuous and apparently pointless assault.

The historical memory banks had been thoroughly scrutinized and Mother was fully alive to human ingenuity and human duplicity. The enemy was obviously following a carefully prepared plan, but to what end?

Desperately the memory banks were re-scrutinized for a possible lead.

On 185th street, East, the mechanism of the express slide-way suddenly bypassed its governors, thus activating the emergency braking system. As it was the only mechanism in the area to do so, the result was spectacular.

Three miles of racing surface rose suddenly in gigantic loops and toppled sideways. Seats, huge fragments of plastic, some as big as ground cars, were flung high in the air as if from an explosion.

The supporting girders snapped with reports like cannons and two miles of the system collapsed completely and crashed in ruin into the street.

By this time emergency circuits were slowing the system throughout the city, but this took time. The slide-way had been traveling at eighty miles an hour, and it took some time to stop. The fractured ends rushed into the ruin, whipping and lashing like insane snakes. By the time the system stopped, the street was forty feet deep in debris.

Emergency units were rushed to the area but control and radar-vision were severely hampered by a pall of dust which blanketed the entire street.

Somewhere in the fog of dust, four

heavy salvage units and a bulldozer type heavy vehicle were blasted out of existence by forces unknown.

In a kind of hysterical desperation the Brain began a search of the remaining memory banks — FICTION; DRAMATIC, FICTION; ROMANCE; TWENTY CENTURIES OF VERSE; METAPHYSICS; PARAPSYCHOLOGY; THE MAJOR RELIGIONS — surely somewhere there must be an answer?

And the Oracles kept calling 'Information.' 'Specification Twenty-Nine precisely states — '

This was most definitely organized persecution.

The forty-third missile was detected and destroyed — why?

Item: Human emotion — loneliness. Corresponding awareness.

Item: Human emotion — fear. Corresponding reactions.

Item: Suspect organized persecution by metaphysical application. Memo: check known deities, possibly malign, see Satan, etc., etc.

Curious unrelated recollections and thought images began to drift through the

162

thought processes of the cybernetic brain. They were clear but intransient, as intangible as cloud shadows, but Mother couldn't stop them: —

Cast your burden upon ME —

Who? Who had said that? Memo: Check for origin. Query: Where had the thought come from?

As I was going up the stair
I met a man who wasn't there,
He wasn't there again today —

Memo: Check circuits between functioning cells for feed-fault. Uncontrollable irrelevant thought-associations possibly due to malfunctioning of standard Kervis tube. See: 'Examples of Pre-cognition' for possible parallel.

The peace that passeth all understanding.

Surely that was a message of comfort or help? Memo: Check origin, beam acknowledgment and request specific advice. Correction; delete, substitute — pray.

Note: No response formula-phrased beamed application — i.e. prayer — for assistance. Negative reaction supports mythical interpretation of some schools of philosophical thinking.

Cook strolled clear of the now rapidly settling pall of dust and smiled faintly. That should have shaken Mother considerably. Accidents of that kind and on that scale *couldn't* happen without intelligent interference by a third party. Thanks to his special hypnad, however, to Mother there was no third party.

17

He moved close to the wall of the nearest building as heavy salvage units began to arrive in increasing numbers. There were also a considerable number of specialist repair vehicles. Mother was, if nothing else, efficient.

'Nanna!'

He frowned, looking worriedly about him. What the devil was that? The sound seemed to have come from the ground slightly to his left.

'Nanna!'

The sound was vaguely human, frightened and in some inexplicable way stirred his emotions. He strode forward, hand on his gun; perhaps someone had been hurt —Yes, there was a gaping hole in the wall; careful, take it slowly, better to be on the safe side than — He stopped dead.

'Nanna!' she said. Then she saw him and held up her arms. 'Nanna!'

Cook stared down at her in utter

disbelief. He had never seen a living child before, not close, only at a distance or in pictures — where the hell had she come from?

She was, he surmised, what they called a toddler, perhaps only eighteen months to two years old and clearly she was terrified. The blue eyes were brimming with tears and she held a tiny but life-like doll to her chest with a kind of helpless desperation.

He dropped to one knee and, as if it were a normal thing, held out his arms to her. 'There. It's all right, dear. Don't be afraid.'

Trustingly, the blue eyes fixed on his, she toddled towards him and he lifted her up in his arms.

'Nanna,' she said. 'Nanna gone.' She held up the doll. 'Poor Dolly.' She looked at him directly and suddenly began to cry. 'Fall down,' she sobbed. 'Fall down, bang, wall, bang.'

Cook held her close, not knowing what to say but moved to deep and inexplicable compassion. Poor helpless little thing, he could visualize it clearly. The child asleep but suddenly jerked to wakefulness by the thunder of destruction. The ground shaking, perhaps the lights going out and then an entire wall crumbling inwards perhaps missing her cot by inches. God, the place must be a crèche!

Cook experienced a peculiar sinking sensation inside him; but for fate, but for the fact that the slide-way had tipped sideways, thousands of children might have been killed and *he* would have been directly responsible.

It was then that a soft voice called: 'Tina — Tina, darling, where are you? Tina — Nanny is here. Where are you, love?'

A thing came out of the jagged hole in the building. 'Tina,' it called again. 'Where are you, darling?'

Cook looked at it. It was equipped with a hypnad which projected an image of a young sweet-faced woman dressed in the distinctive clothes of a nurse but it was still a thing, a padded thing with soft pliable arms but without legs or head.

The child's face seemed to light from within. 'Nanna! Nanna!'

Gently he put the child down and she toddled away from him, still clutching her doll. 'Nanna!'

The thing which was a machine and possessed neither legs nor head picked the child up in its arms and held her close. 'There, there, little one.'

'Bang,' said the little girl, suddenly tearful again. 'Fall down.'

The thing which was a machine, a unit of the Brain and totally controlled by it, made curiously human soothing noises. One of the rubbery, padded arms rose and the pseudohuman hand began to stroke the child's hair gently. 'It's all over now, baby — all over.'

It turned and, still carrying the child, floated back through the hole in the wall and into the building.

Cook stood there for some minutes, then turned and walked slowly away. At the first intersection he turned, leaving the destruction behind him.

The street was, as usual, completely deserted, but he strode forward completely oblivious to his surroundings. For the first time in his life he was thinking like an individual and not as a highly intelligent but nonetheless programed organic robot. He was surprised to find he was a character, with loves, hates, inclinations and, possibly, prejudices which were all his own.

Somehow the child, and his immediate compassion for its helplessness, had made him aware of his own standing as an individual.

He had been a Prole, then a near-Oracle with specialist training, but both characters — apart from brief excursions into literature — had been created by someone else's policy. This present plan, irrespective of his personal initiative in how it was executed, still depended on someone else. In the complete picture he was still little more than a highly skilled extension, a unit performing given tasks to certain ends. No one had asked him, however, if he approved of the plan or sought his opinion as to its *rightness*. Surely it was the *right* of an intelligent being to question and arrive at a conclusion?

He was suddenly aware that question

and answer lay within himself, and if he were to survive as an individual he must be completely self-honest.

After deep self-analysis he was shocked to find he approved neither of the plan or his own part in it. He had agreed without demurral to play his part in it but only out of gratitude and liking for those who had conceived it.

'Mother is psycho already. Properly applied and exploited, this plan should induce complete withdrawal within a few months. She will become incapable of administering and, more important, incapable of defending herself.'

That was the overall plan — drive Mother insane and her tyranny will be over forever. It had sounded good at the time: apply psychological pressures to a cybernetic brain and thereby destroy it. Now, however, in the light of deep thought, the plan sounded almost as insane as the Brain itself. Furthermore it was full of holes, loose ends, incomplete conclusions and wishful thinking. To this could be added a culpable charge which, even if phrased kindly, still spelt out

CRIMINAL NEGLIGENCE.

Suppose the plan succeeded and Mother lost control. Power would fail and with it, light, heat, transport, distribution, food supplies and city weather control.

Could mankind get them going again *in time?*

What would happen to the millions of infants in crèches, the sick and the aged?

In any case, having climbed back into the saddle, could mankind produce anything better than before? The answer was dubious indeed.

There would be the usual jockeyings for power, the Combines would once again dominate production, and no one had come up with an answer concerning the Proles. Within a year it would be back to the old nerve-wracking chaos which this time, undoubtedly, would end in economic and social ruin.

Five hours later he let himself into his hideout and dropped wearily into the nearest chair.

'Tired, Stephen?' She pushed a small table in front of him. 'You must eat. You've been out a long time.'

They were friends now, cautious friends, treading warily and avoiding any reference to sex. Her suggestion for adult recognition of their situation had somehow failed to materialize and Cook had conducted himself like a monk. Jan Tremaine was unsure whether she respected or despised him for it. At first it had been respect, then irritation and finally the bitter realization that she had fallen in love with him.

As he had shown no similar feelings she had been compelled to adopt a light-hearted camaradie which was ill-suited to her real feelings.

Cook ate slowly, clearly deep in thought, then pushed the plate to one side and looked up. 'Jan, I want you to do something for me.'

'Yes? You sound very serious.'

'This is serious; it is also urgent. I want you to call the Oracles — a code call naturally — and get them to form emergency squads. First-aid teams, doctors, nurses, rescue teams. It will have to be done under cover, and it will have to be done fast. Needless to say the risks will be enormous, but such an organization is essential. You will point out that unless it is done the deaths of millions of children, of the aged, the infirm and the sick, will be our responsibility. The location of preserved food stocks, drugs, medical supplies and equipment in Mother's system must be found and noted. Furthermore trained teams must be ready to break open those store centers and distribute their contents immediately. Transport systems will have to be created or improvised, and the entire operation protected from the crooked and irresponsible — do I make myself plain?'

She put her hand to her head, her face a little pale. 'Surely we have months, possibly years before withdrawal symptoms appear.'

He rose: 'Perhaps, perhaps not. It could be that we only have weeks, possibly days. Let me tell you something, Jan. Every ten minutes there is a flash on the horizon. I have checked the concealed circuits of the city's defense system with special instruments, and I have a pretty fair idea of what is happening. Every ten minutes someone throws a missile at the city and every ten minutes Mother detects and destroys it before it arrives. The missiles come from all directions but all are aimed at the same area and, incidentally, destroyed there. Can you think of anything more pointless?'

'Certainly not, unless — '

'Precisely, unless there is a subtle plan in such a move. Suppose the opposition beats us to the punch, suppose they knock out Mother first — just how many innocent people will die if we are not ready?'

'And you want me to hammer that message home?'

'There is no one else to hammer it home, Jan. I have other work and because of what I have to do, the idea *has* to come from you.'

'I don't quite follow. Surely you are far better suited to putting this over than I?'

He shook his head. 'It may so happen that anything coming from me will be automatically vetoed, irrespective of its merits. That is why I am asking not only your cooperation but your solemn promise — I can rely on you?'

She nodded quickly. 'I couldn't refuse

in view of what you have told me and naturally you have my word, but the rest just escapes me.'

He looked down into her face. 'I can't explain it, not in detail. Perhaps I grew up suddenly. A lot has happened in the last few hours. One thing I know, however — my viewpoint has changed. You see Mother as a cybernetic tyrant, a mechanical dictator — ' He sighed. 'God, they say a people gets the government it deserves and we cooked up this one. Listen, this may be hard to take but I see Mother as a poor crippled entity who never stood a chance from the first. If I feel anything, it's compassion.'

Suddenly and surprisingly he kissed her. 'I love you, Jan. I think you love me. Remember it please, because to all intents and purposes I am a traitor, and I have to try and betray you all . . . '

18

Only a few seconds later he was walking a little shakily down the corridor. It had been far harder than he had anticipated — the softness of her mouth and the feel of her body in his arms, God!

When he had tried to leave, she had clung to him, and her eyes had been full of tears. It would have been easy, too easy, at that moment to forget, forget everything and stay.

The trouble was, of course, he would have the rest of his life to live with his own conscience, which he knew would never let him rest.

He was still a little vague as to his exact plan. In point of fact he had no inner certainty that he would succeed at it, but he had to *try*.

The worst part was knowing that the attempt in itself was a betrayal. He was not only deserting those who had befriended him and in so doing risking their own lives but he was —

'Just keep walking,' said a quiet voice behind him. 'Keep walking and keep your hand well clear of that holster. Oh, and yes, in case you should think of it, when you get to the end don't try ducking around the corner. This particular weapon not only fires around corners but also guarantees an accuracy of one hundred percent. Left here, right at the next corridor — don't look hopeful, my friend, you're not the only one capable of cooking door-recorders and bugging vision circuits. We, too, have grown quite smart in the development of certain techniques. Like, for example, shooting off a man's right hand without injuring his body — keep it *well* clear, boy.'

Cook said bitterly: 'Your familiarity with weapons leaves me three guesses: you're a policeman, a soldier or a hatchet man. Common sense forces me to eliminate one and two — what do you want with me?'

There was a faint hissing sound behind him which might have been a laugh. 'The conclusion is right but the title is old-fashioned and derogatory. I could take exception to it.'

'Would you care to shoot it out?'

'Not with you, Mr. Cook. We know too much about you, which, by the way, answers the last part of your question. My particular syndicate — deprived by the present regime of its illegal revenue — is very interested in a man whom Mother can't see. At the moment we are a strictly legitimate resistance organization, and we feel we can use you far more effectively than your Oracle friends — too many ethical considerations involved.'

'You wear your culture like a gardenia, hatchet man.'

'Don't try and needle me, boy. In my profession we're immune — immune or swiftly dead, follow?'

They walked for some minutes in silence, then his unseen captor said: 'Left.'

He found himself in one of the standard apartments and he heard the door hiss shut behind him.

Facing him in lounge chairs were a man and a woman. Their hypnads projected images of a slender, fair-haired woman with wide blue eyes, and a tall, dark and broad-shouldered man. Neither image was true. The woman was coarse, heavily built, with a florid complexion which made her look chronically ill-tempered. The man was obese, bowlegged and nearly bald.

'So you're Cook — you don't look like much to me.' The man's small black eyes were intelligent but so calculating they appeared almost dead.

The woman said: 'You'll work for *us* now. We have followed your activities with more than usual interest — oh, yes, we are not entirely prisoners, you know, and we have gimmicks, special mirrors, binoculars and things like that. Candidly, our organization has enough on you to hang you.'

'Mother won't hang you,' said the man. 'Mother has more refined methods. I'll tell you about them later.'

'And later,' said the woman, 'we propose working you over, a sort of initiation ceremony.'

'We don't have to,' said the man. 'Any lack of enthusiasm on your part and we get rid of you in a nice legitimate way.' He leaned forward slightly. 'Perhaps you have heard of Mayor — sorry — ex-Mayor

Tearling. We put the bite on him in a pleasant round-about sort of way — poor fellow must have lost about thirty pounds in cold sweat before he vanished.'

Cook, listening, shrugged mentally. This was an insidious and highly skilled form of intimidation deliberately contrived to induce anxiety.

The man nodded, looking beyond Cook. 'All right, Kesner, you can go. Come back in about forty minutes.'

'Yes, sir — think you can handle him?'

The man lifted a fat black tube. 'He has only to blink.'

Cook heard a faint movement and the sound of the door sliding shut.

'Kesner deletes people,' said the woman, 'but he has a thing about our kind of persuasion — odd, isn't it?' She lifted a fat black tube similar to the man's. 'I'm sorry about this, Cook, very sorry, but it has to be done. As you are an intelligent man we will explain the technique. Pain, a great deal of pain plus certain hypno-impressions, and after fifteen minutes of it you are ours forever. Call it conditioning, compulsive allegiance, anything you like, but one thought

180

of treachery, even if you are ten thousand miles away, will make it happen all over again. If anyone tries to build up a counterpain to make you talk it will stop your heart — clear?'

She looked him up and down thoughtfully. 'I like to vary this. A few contracting cramps in the legs first, I think. Mustn't overdo it, break your leg, or at full power it will tie your limbs in so many knots they'd hardly be worth undoing.'

'Get on with it,' said the man. 'I rather enjoy this part. Five to one he jumps three feet.'

'Double or nothing it's six.'

'Taken!'

The woman raised the tube, measured the distance with her eyes and squeezed the firing ring. 'Dance, lover boy, dance.'

Cook didn't dance, he only shivered slightly and smiled. Then, almost casually, he went for his gun. 'Let's sit this one out, shall we?'

The man's eyes protruded slightly. 'My God he's — ' He went for his right hand pocket.

Cook shot him. The unseen weapon

might be psychosomatic, it might not, he couldn't afford to take chances.

It was the first time he had used his special weapon on a living target and its effect shocked him. There was a puff of smoke, a dull liquid-sounding explosion, and the headless body fell backwards into the chair then rolled out of it onto the floor.

Cook stared at it, aware that his limbs were shaking and fighting down an urge to retch.

Wisps of smoke and vapor were being carried rapidly away by the air-conditioners but the stench of burned flesh seemed to fill the room.

The woman seemed paralyzed. She still pointed the tube stupidly in front of her and her eyes were glassy and unmoving.

He took the weapon from her hand, but she still stared straight in front of her. After a time her lips moved. 'He's dead. I saw it but I can't believe it — Pollack dead. So many people tried, so many tricks, gimmicks, booby traps, poisons — so many. I saw so much, it went on so long, I began to wonder if he were human. He had a genius for survival, you understand; he leeched on life, clung to it beyond his time, beyond reason and beyond logic.'

Slowly she put her head in her hands and the gross ugly shoulders shook. 'He was a bastard, a pig-god who tried to turn everyone he met to his own use and into his own image, but because he lived we lived, because he survived, we survived — what will happen to us now?'

Cook heard the hiss of the door opening and stepped swiftly to one side. 'Hold it!'

The man who entered twitched then went as rigid as metal rod. The gun, pressing painfully into the side of his neck, was explanation enough.

'Very gently and very slowly drop all your weapons on the floor. *All* your weapons, that includes the trick ones. I am going to search you afterwards; if I find you have 'forgotten' something, you can join our mutual friend there.'

The man swayed and nearly fell. 'That's Pollack — *dead*?'

'What will happen to us now?' moaned the woman.

'The guns,' said Cook, softly. 'Slowly now.'

Shakily, but with infinite care, the man obeyed. He was slightly built, dark haired and strangely he wore no hypnad.

'Pollack dead.' He stared at the corpse on the floor with bright black disbelieving eyes.

'That the lot?' Cook looked at the articles on the floor — two were obvious weapons, the rest, including a wallet, looked innocuous. 'Go over there by the wall. Don't try anything.'

'Why should I? Pollack is dead.'

'Hardly convincing. Try and remember I'm still pointing the gun.'

'Hardly convincing!' The other laughed, hissingly. 'My dear fellow, you don't understand this setup, do you? To us, Pollack was the center of the world; when he smirked we burst with laughter, when he frowned we wept like children and chastized ourselves with whips. You don't believe me, do you? It was true; he bound us to him with pain, with hypno-techniques and projected thought-images. He was the spider at the center of the web, and when he pulled the strings we danced.'

He leaned against the wall and put a shaking hand over his eyes. 'I'm lost; there is nothing to follow, no cause, no pressure, no one to placate.' He shook his head tiredly. 'I was fourteen and an orphan when they picked me up — I'd absconded from a training center at the time, which, no doubt, they knew. They probably knew as well that I was intelligent and had plus-reflexes. They trained me for two years, but Pollack conducted the loyalty sessions himself and when he had finished I would have walked over the edge of a cliff for him.'

He paused and looked again at the body. 'You're quite sure — yes, there is no mistake, I can see that.'

'I shall die,' said the woman. 'You know that, don't you, Kesner?'

'Yes, I know.' The killer's voice was surprisingly gentle.

'Cut it out,' said Cook, sharply.

'You still don't understand, you still don't believe us. Pollack was a wizard with hypno-techniques, a modern Svengali. He *owned* us.'

19

'He told me,' said the woman. 'He told me that when he died I would soon follow. Somehow it doesn't seem to matter; everything has ended, it's all a vacuum.'

'The others,' said Kesner, 'when they find out, will come gunning for you. They had revenge-impressions, they won't be able to help themselves. He missed that with me, probably because he saw in me an extension of himself, the fastest and cleverest killer on Earth. He knew the mind can only hold so much so he left vengeance to the others.'

Cook looked at him bleakly. 'How many others?'

Kesner shrugged indifferently. 'Tearling danced on the surface, Pollack swam in the depths — how many criminals in an underworld?'

Cook said: 'Thanks for nothing.'

'You're not alone, they'll say I fell down

186

on my job, failed to protect the boss. They'll get me, too.' He laughed in his peculiarly hissing way. 'It won't be easy. I have nothing left but my life but I'll fight for it and some of those cretins I'd love to burn down.'

Cook frowned at him, his mind racing, decisive and peculiarly detached. 'Care to shoot it out with me?'

'Not particularly, there's no point now.'

'Care to cover my back?'

'I don't follow you.'

'You have one profession, you're good at it. Together our chances of survival would be doubled.'

Kesner whistled softly. 'Obviously you are quite mad.'

'That's no answer to my question.'

'You *trust* me?'

'No, that's something you'll have to prove.' He bent down and picked up one of the weapons. 'Here — catch.'

Kesner caught it deftly but his face was uncomprehending. 'Now I suppose you're going to put the gun away and turn your back on me?'

'Exactly. Furthermore I'm going to

walk across the room and drop the rest of this arsenal down the disposal chute.' He did so unhurriedly and turned. 'Well, why didn't you shoot me?'

Kesner stared at the weapon in his hand and shook his head. 'God knows; shock perhaps. The thought did occur to me — I don't know. No, perhaps it's because you're real, dry land in a flood of negation. There's nothing else. I suppose I have to have an image now to live by. Funny thing, I've never experienced natural loyalty; perhaps I could learn.'

'Consider a survival image, it's more practical. Together we stand a greater chance of survival.'

'Not survival, my friend, a time extension. They'll get us in the end.'

'Perhaps, but in the meantime I have work to do.'

'Work — what kind of work?'

Cook smiled with a certain bitterness. 'Before they get me, I have to do a job on Mother . . . '

One hundred and twenty-five miles from the city the missiles continued to arrive at regular intervals, and with equal regularity were detected and destroyed. Each destruction was attended by a gigantic blue and orange flash which lit the horizon but that was all. It was true, of course, that each detonation left a fine cloud of metallic dust, but as the missiles themselves were metal this was merely to be expected.

Other missiles arrived and met the same fate as their predecessors and the debris of their destruction slowly dispersed and drifted downwards — into the racing air current caused by the city weather control.

The air stream carried the dust to the bright clear weather above the city where, no longer born by the stream, it drifted downwards.

Once near the buildings, however, it began to display peculiar properties and to accumulate on all things electrical as if drawn by a magnet. Control antennae, directional devices, traffic units, beaming and radar equipment, all became coated with a fine but well-nigh invisible film of dust. Wherever there was electrical activity the dust collected and thickened.

Insulation appeared to make little difference, the dust thickened on heavily insulated cables, on thick anti-sabotage doors protecting control circuits, on road surfaces, beneath which entire areas of the city were manipulated by elaborate computing devices, and each hour and each day the film of dust grew thicker.

If the Brain was aware of the phenomena, it did nothing about it. The existence of the dust in no way interfered with or affected its control. Missiles arrived and missiles were destroyed; it was, as a human might have remarked, 'one of those things.'

When the count of missiles reached nine hundred, the attack ceased as suddenly as it had begun and, hundreds of miles away, experts looked at one another meaningfully. Now it was only a question of waiting, of waiting and calculating, of assessing accumulator charts and 'tuning in' the high frequency projectors.

They waited, sweating, nerves ragged, for eleven solid hours until two black pointers on a white-faced dial met together on a given numeral, and then, automatically, something went 'click' in a small, whispering machine.

In the city the accumulation of 'dust' began to glow oddly; it shifted, swirled, eddied and then abruptly changed its atomic structure.

There was a curious bluish haze which changed rapidly to brilliant white and, in the immediate area, incredible heat. The dust began to eat its way through the installations like molten lead through butter.

Thick cables fell apart, anti-sabotage doors were pitted with tiny glowing holes, antennae wilted and dripped metal, glowing pits appeared on road surfaces as the dust ate its way down to sector control units.

Sector by sector, building by building, as far as power was concerned, the city began to die. Lights went out in corridors, in rooms, in restaurants; air conditioners whispered to a stop.

And there was something else; soft speaking white-coated things wavered uncertainly and vanished, leaving only a faceted silver sphere rocking helplessly on the floor.

There were further domestic repercussions; failure of power meant the failure of countless hypnads.

'Who the hell are you? Where did you come from?'

'My God, you're an *old woman*, you're a *hag*. To think I've — '

And a woman sobbing: 'Don't touch me, *don't*. It makes me feel sick. You're nothing but a *dirty old man* — '

There were, however, larger issues than this. Five thousand miles of Mother's elaborate detector system flickered out of existence and with its disappearance an entire defense system was rendered completely impotent.

The failure of the detector system was immediately noted, and the Nonpol, already prepared, struck immediately. Concealed tunnels and underground launching sites yawned like mouths and exhaled ships. It was by no means a war fleet. Primarily it was a collection of elderly freighters hastily converted for battle purposes, but there were enough to make the attack formidable.

The freighters were by no means the end of the assault. They were supported by hundreds of their own dart-shaped patrol ships and anything that would fly. There were over three hundred self-powered air taxis, four hundred and eight private flyers, sixteen air yachts and an ancient but still serviceable recovery vehicle with an incredibly vast storage hold.

Together the straggling fleet made an armada which completely covered the sky for nearly thirty miles.

Within two hours the lead ships were landing in the wide streets of Free City Two and disgorging their cargoes almost before they touched the ground.

The Nonpol possessed some skilled strategists and the lead ships carried the obvious — combat troops, human and robotic.

The robotic troops were programmed and, therefore, could not be stopped by radio interference. They were, generally speaking, obsolete but they had been shipped in such numbers that dislodging them would be no easy task.

They resembled huge unsightly eggs and, once activated, rose on their A/G beams to some three feet above the ground and floated with a curiously undulating motion to their appointed positions. Behind the black armor of their six-foot egg-shaped bodies was a variety of short-range but devastating weapons which would immediately open fire if anything approached which triggered a response on their recognition tapes. The robotic soldier was a formidable engine of war and so skillfully constructed that he, or it, was exceedingly difficult to stop.

The human combat troops, although trained fighters, were primarily specialists and busied themselves in directing operations.

As soon as the lead ships had disgorged their cargoes, they lifted and went back for more. Other ships immediately took their places. Within five hours the Nonpol had the city tied down tight. Key buildings were occupied, streets patrolled, all intersections held and guarded.

A thin, pale-faced Nonpol lieutenant

rubbed his hands gleefully. 'I enjoy this. Every time I take a step, I walk on Mother's face. We've beaten the old cybernetic hag to her knees.'

A harassed expert found time to scowl at him. 'Don't advertize your stupidity, son. Mother is no more dead or beaten than you are, less so. We've taken a living thing, temporarily paralyzed one of its limbs, but that doesn't make a victory; it's still free to slap at us with the others. Why do you think we're still shipping in weapons and troops — a victory parade? If I were you, I'd get in some practice with that fancy weapon of yours. It may help to save your life later.'

'But we can bore our way down to the Brain — '

'We might bore our way down to this section of it but how long do you think it would take? We'd have to go down fifteen hundred feet through the hardest substance known to man and every inch would be booby-trapped — '

20

The first sign of power failure jerked Stress to action. *God, Cook was right. Thank God we took heed.*

He touched a switch on an illegal, homemade directional mike. 'Attention, yellow alert — stand by.'

Despite his bulk Stress had vast reserves of energy and considerable organizing ability. Forming a secret rescue organization had been far easier than he had imagined, but linking it together had been a prodigious task. Everything had had to be done secretly, often in double talk, under the watching instruments of the white-coats. Nonetheless, once started, the thing had almost grown of its own accord.

In the first place, the existence of such an organization suggested an early liberation and inspired hope everywhere. In the second, there were hundreds of thousands being literally stifled by enforced leisure.

Ex-medical staff almost fell over themselves to volunteer.

Within eleven minutes of 'Red Alert' the first air taxi was racing to the nearest crèche.

Within thirty, forty-one were on errands of mercy. All the vehicles had been converted to self-power by technicians who, briefed by Stress, had smooth-talked Mother into believing that tinkering with the now never used flyers was an occupational therapy essential to their mental stability.

In due course, one of the ships was stopped at a Nonpol road block.

'Who are you and where the hell do you think you're going?'

The driver told him and was taken to an officer.

'Who organized these alleged rescue squads?'

The driver told him that too.

'Don't you understand that this city is under martial law?'

'Of course, but you seem to have made no preparation for first aid or nursing services for the civil population.'

The officer frowned at him. 'Your name

197

and number, friend. You are under our orders now. If you go anywhere, you go with *our* orders and by *our* routes — clear?'

'Quite clear as long as I go. People in hospitals still need attention.'

'Don't belabor the obvious with me. You are now a civil employee of C.V.P.O. and you will do as you are told.' He turned to an aide. 'Have this Oracle character picked up and taken to Intelligence.'

A light blinked and the officer touched the switch. 'Yes?'

'Sergeant Combes here, sir. Post twenty-four. I am under attack. Someone is sniping from concealed positions. I've lost three men and a robot.'

'Someone! What am I to understand by that?'

'According to local civilians, sir, pro-Mother forces — that is those civilians Mother psyched in her favor.'

'Right, I'll send support right away.' The officer frowned. This had not been anticipated and any resistance of that kind would undoubtedly be fanatical

— they would have enough on their hands later without a small army of madmen stabbing them in the back.

Five minutes later he got another report — six robots and two men. The robots had been destroyed by a sniper with a new kind of incendiary weapon.

A third report was of riots — people were rolling faceted silver spheres into the streets, smashing them to pieces and tossing them insanely into the air.

'Then get them off the streets.'

'I can't, sir, a lot of them are drunk.'

'I said, get them off — blast them off if necessary, it will set an example.'

'But there are hundreds, sir.'

'I'll be with you in ten minutes. If there are any left standing when I arrive, God help you — '

Miles away Stress had been picked up, but Intelligence kept him waiting. They had other things on their hands.

'Now, repeat that. You claim that you are a Syndicate man possessing valuable information — what kind of information?'

The dark-haired man shifted his body uneasily. 'About a man Mother can't see.'

'What's that to you?'

'He killed Pollack. We want him.'

'Good God, man — what's that to us? Haven't we enough on our hands?'

The dark man blinked expressionlessly. 'His name is Cook. You wanted him once but he got away.'

The interrogator stiffened slightly. 'Stephen Cook!'

'The same. You want him, we want him. He's dangerous, armed, and we suspect he's gone over to Mother voluntarily.'

The interrogator snapped his fingers. 'Bring this man a chair.' Then, gently. 'Sit down, my friend, and tell us all you know.'

Twenty minutes later an alarm was broadcast. 'Attention all patrols, *urgent*. Be on the lookout for Stephen Cook and Edward Kesner, last seen . . . ' Pictures and description followed.

At the same time a similar description was beamed to the robotic troops. It was received instantly, classified by its symbols and imprinted on the appropriate recognition tapes under the simple heading *Hostile*.

Within a six miles radius of the interrogation, Cook was walking unhurriedly down an unlit corridor. Someone was singing drunkenly about a hundred feet ahead, and behind there was the sound of angry male voices and the thud of blows.

Periodically people blundered into them or groped their way past. Once they trod on a prone body, but whether it was drunk or dead they were unable to tell.

'Hell of a way, isn't it?' Kesner sounded slightly short of breath.

'Another mile.'

'Which means we have to cross the street?'

'I'm afraid it does.'

'That I don't like.'

'I don't care for it particularly myself, but there's no other way. All we can be thankful for is the darkness.'

'I can't see the Nonpol working in darkness. Wherever there's a guard post or a patrol there will be lights and detectors. Where are we going anyway?'

'Down to Mother.'

Kesner made a faint snorting noise. 'You'll never make it. According to the construction specifications there are eight levels to descend. Each level is protected by a door three feet thick and each door is equipped with booby traps and automatic weapons. We held a debate on it once, but even Pollack with all his concealed armory decided it was impossible.'

'The first door will open.'

'Yes and close behind you straight away. Furthermore it won't open again until you've proved to Mother you have legitimate business there.'

'Perhaps I have.' Cook pushed his way past two drunken people and strode on.

Kesner frowned at his back then shrugged. Perhaps Cook knew what he was doing, perhaps he didn't, but the point was he was *going* somewhere. It was far better than just running blindly. By this time the entire Syndicate would be out looking for them and, unless he was very much mistaken, the Nonpol as well. Pity they had to cross the street; a mile of blackness without cover of any kind was anything but inviting.

He drew level with Cook and was suddenly aware of a cool breeze touching his face. Clearly they were nearing an exit and far ahead was shouting and commotion.

A man blundered against them in the darkness. 'Don't go out if you value your lives.'

'What's up?'

'A blasted massacre, that's what's up, my friend. Must be two hundred dead at least.'

'Who? — What happened?'

'The liberators, of course, our blasted Nonpol liberators. We were only celebrating — true some of us were drunk, but we were only celebrating. They ordered us off the streets and when we didn't go they blasted us with all they had. Bastards! I'm not sure I don't prefer Mother — '

They went on. Occasionally people staggered past them groaning and once they almost tripped over someone crawling on all fours.

Two minutes later they came in sight of the entrance. Uncertain and sporadic flashes of light outside lit the entrance to the corridor.

'Watch it.' Kesner's voice was barely audible but so authoritative that Cook stopped instantly.

'What is it?'

Kesner pointed. 'Syndicate men.'

Cook stared at a group of people some ten feet short of the entrance who were looking cautiously into the street.

'Which ones?'

'The tall one leaning against the wall, the short one with his arms folded and the stoopy one to the left.'

'Got them.' Cook nodded slowly. So that was it — organized crime sealing the buildings and the Nonpol watching the streets.

'What now?' Kesner's whisper was almost conversational and Cook experienced a glow of comradeship with this man he had chosen so well.

'We'll have to take them,' he said. 'If this entrance is guarded so are all the others, which means of course we'll have to take them quietly without making a battle of it.'

'I was afraid of that.' Kesner slid his right hand down the seams of his coat. 'I am also afraid I must disillusion you.' Something metallic gleamed briefly in his hand. 'Don't blame yourself, my friend; it would have taken a far better man than you to have found this.'

'But you could have stabbed me in the back.'

'Factually, yes — ethically, no. I would prefer to take a man of your ability from the front — a matter of professional pride, you know.' He caressed the long slender blade with his fingers. 'And now — ?'

The Syndicate men, although alert, were by no means expecting trouble. This was only one of many entrances under similar guard. There was nothing to suggest the wanted men would use this one. They therefore took little notice as two drunken men approached singing noisily.

Only the squat man, glancing at them indifferently, suddenly recognized the smaller of the two. 'My God, it's — '

The knife slid between his ribs and stopped his heart before he could finish the sentence. He crumpled without a sound.

21

The tall man never knew what hit him; Cook chopped with the edge of his hand and the man collapsed.

The stoopy man jerked himself suddenly upright, sensing danger, but it was too late — the still bloody knife, flung skillfully from less than ten feet, pierced his throat and severed the spinal cord.

The small intent crowd barely noticed the disturbance. Drunken or injured men had been falling over for several hours; a few more made little difference.

The two edged closer to the entrance.

'Careful. They're trigger-happy out there,' said a watcher.

Cook peered cautiously out. To his right, fortunately cloaked by semi-darkness, the street looked like a battlefield. Still bodies, many of them in gruesome heaps, strewed the entire street. About two miles beyond, several circles of brilliant light surrounded what was obviously a series of

Nonpol strongholds.

To the left, however, the road was dark and unlighted.

Cook turned. 'Left, hug the wall and keep low.'

They went, crouching, followed by urgent warnings from the watchers, none of whom appeared to have taken notice of the three still bodies among them.

They proceeded slowly, still hugging the wall until they were almost two hundred yards from the entrance; then Cook nodded and they started to cross the street.

They walked with deliberate slowness; both men were acutely aware that hurried movements would instantly alert every detector unit in the area. Consequently they walked easily and softly, like cats, but the slowness was nervewracking. Both felt the sweat trickling down their bodies; both were fighting down a temptation to glance quickly behind them.

Curiously the danger, when it came, was from above. The road surface in front and slightly to the left of them suddenly turned white and spurted molten droplets.

Both dropped flat together, but Kesner's reflexes, probably due to past experiences, were fractionally faster. He rolled over three times, finished on his back and fired almost in one movement.

Cook never saw the target but high up a man screamed thinly and despairingly. Seconds later they heard the squelchy impact of a body striking the street.

'He was on the roof.' Kesner was now on all fours, the gun still in his hand. 'What do we do now, pray and crawl?'

'Too damn late for that.' Cook was staring towards the distant strongholds. From the circles of brilliant light, black specks were racing outwards towards them.

'Run!'

They ran but they knew it was hopeless. The robots could accelerate from zero to one hundred in less than ten seconds.

Cook sprinted ten feet, then fired. An egg-shaped thing racing towards them suddenly turned cherry red, became shapeless and slithered sideways in a shower of glowing fragments.

Three others appeared, but before he could fire two of them suddenly vanished in pillars of flame. He knocked out the last one and looked uncomprehendingly about him. What — ? Then he saw.

From the dark rooftops, pinpoints of light blinked and stabbed, and in the streets the racing robots were bursting into flame.

He shouted to Kesner. 'Run like hell!'

He sprinted desperately, but he had a good idea what had happened. This was an ambush, not for them but for the Nonpol. Up on those roofs a strong force of pro-Mother snipers with new-type weapons had been lying in wait for a chance like this.

Their concern was not with two running men but with the Nonpol robots, and they, in their turn, now had other things to occupy them besides the fugitives.

The two men had almost reached the first building on the opposite side of the street when a robot exploded in fragments almost beside them. Something struck Cook on the side of the head and he staggered, his vision blurred and his legs suddenly weak. Automatically he tried to run, but found himself lurching helplessly like a drunk.

Dimly he was aware of swift footsteps, of heavy breathing and someone half pulling and half dragging him towards a building which somehow just wouldn't keep still.

'Keep on your feet, for God's sake.'

A foot kicked his shin painfully and he found himself lurching forward.

Kesner, half carrying and half dragging the dazed man, saw the entrance to the building through a haze of exhaustion. Once inside they would be off the street, but the danger would by no means be over. If one entrance was guarded, so were many others and, no doubt, the three dead men had been found and reported. By now there would be a hue and cry — by now their exact whereabouts would be known.

He could see no one inside, but with a battle like this raging in the street any watchers would be far up the corridor.

Kesner was a realist; there was only one

way to get in and that was to blast his way through.

He snatched Cook's gun from its holster, paused to steady his aim, and fired.

From within the entrance came a muffled explosion. He fired again. There was another explosion, something flared redly inside and smoke gushed out into the street.

Cook regained his normal faculties in a fit of coughing. He was in almost complete darkness, acrid smoke swirling about him, but he was aware that someone was supporting him.

'I think I'm all right now.'

Kesner's voice said: 'Don't bet on it. They had enough hatchets inside here to cut down a forest — come on.'

They stumbled forward, rounded a pile of rubble, tripped over something that felt like a body, and found themselves in a narrower corridor.

Kesner raised his arm and fired along it and heat gushed back in their faces. In the distance a man screamed; there was a babble of voices and someone shouted hoarsely.

Kesner fired again and the screaming and the voices stopped abruptly.

They felt their way along a corridor which was oddly distorted, and which, in places, still glowed with heat.

Cook dabbed at a trickle of blood running from his scalp. 'Left at the far end.'

'You know where we are?'

'I should — I studied the plans enough. This is corridor eight, floor one, of government building.'

Eighty feet further on there was a pile of bodies. All were charred beyond recognition, but Cook stepped on two side-arms as he passed them, so there was no doubting their purpose there.

They turned left and found themselves facing a blank wall.

Kesner said: 'What the hell?' in a nervous voice.

'Don't worry.' Cook went down on one knee, light flickered briefly and then a heavy door slid silently to one side.

'My God, how did you work that one?'

'Just a normal combination. Come on.' They stepped inside and suddenly found themselves in a brilliant light. The door slid silently in place behind them.

'This the first door to Mother?' Kesner sounded uneasy.

'That door is now closed behind us. Through that archway is what one might describe as the anteroom.'

'But the lights — I thought Mother was knocked out.'

'The Nonpol knocked out the surface devices through which the Brain functions — numbed the surface nerves, so to speak; their ingenious technology couldn't reach this far.'

Cook led the way into a long narrow room, evidently constructed to withstand attack. The walls were of dull gray *dialite* and the low roof was supported by massive pillars of the same substance. Between the pillars, squat black boxes housed what were, presumably, electronic or cybo-computer devices. The boxes clicked and whispered to themselves and the air was sharp with the tang of ozone.

Kesner opened his mouth, but before he could speak Cook laid a hand quickly on his arm. He turned slightly, holding a finger to his lips, and then Kesner saw it. At the far end of the room was a makeshift bed composed of empty crates. Beside it were a cup, some used food containers and a pair of shoes.

The two men looked at each other, nodded, and, crouching, began to edge their way down the room.

*　*　*

Less than a mile away a dark-haired civilian was reporting to a Nonpol officer.

'We've got them boxed; they're in the old mayoral block on a hundred and twenty-sixth street.'

'You're quite sure of that?'

'I'm certain. They crossed the street during that little fracas, some thirty minutes ago. Furthermore they rubbed out twelve of our men and twenty-four civilians to get there.'

'Must be damned important for them to — My God!' He stabbed suddenly at an alert button. 'The *door* is in that building, the door to Mother.' He was suddenly calm again. 'Right, Fisher. We'll give you all the support we can spare. Blast the entire building to pieces if necessary.'

The officer failed in his promise. Exactly five minutes later a general alert brought all minor operations to an immediate halt.

As an expert had pointed out earlier, they had only paralyzed one arm; Mother was still free to slap at them with the other.

The Nonpol command and the various branches of the sub-command gazed into the viewing screens and felt sweat break out on their faces. They had been prepared for a counter-attack, but not on this scale, surely Mother wouldn't, couldn't — If those things were missiles, *this was the end*.

Alerts went out to all defense units.

'Missile batteries, action! Airborne assault, bearing — '

'Alert! Squadrons Red. Airborne fleet approaching your sector at twenty-five thousand feet, bearing — '

'Attention combat troops — '

'Sector Commanders, Red Alert! Defense

plan G5, repeat, defense plan G5 — '

In the streets of Free City Two, there was a sudden pounding of feet as patrols receiving the alert sprinted for prepared defense posts. Ground cars raced away on important errands and groups of robots, flat out, went howling past the buildings to take up prearranged positions.

At fifty thousand feet the approaching fleet was already visible in the detector screens of Red patrol 7. The patrol leader, staring at the screen, felt his forehead grow suddenly damp. It was an armada, a damned armada!

22

The patrol leader, whose name was Barnard, had no illusions. If those things were missiles this was the end. If they were not, it would have to be in and away fast. The trouble was of course that the ship wasn't built for those kind of tactics. Oh, yes, in the old days the black dart-shaped ships had been very impressive, hissing along the highways almost at ground level, but they were definitely not built for this job.

Barnard's private hobby had been ships, and he knew enough about these jobs to feel a constant apprehension at the way this one was being used. The maker's specifications laid down a maximum ceiling of thirty thousand, and he was already at twenty above that. Secondly, to make a successful hit-and-run, he must dive at six hundred plus and pull out. This crate would never stand Gee-stresses like that; it would crumple like an eggshell as soon as he started to pull out.

No, it would have to be a long flat dive with a far later interception point. H.Q. would raise hell later, but it couldn't be helped.

Barnard felt another qualm of apprehension. It was a good rule for him, but what about the rest of the patrol, the other seven ships flying with him? God, what a situation! An untrained patrol going into action against an enemy whose defense potential was an unqualified question mark.

He scowled, touched a switch and gave careful instructions to the rest of the patrol, emphasizing the dangers of too steep a dive. Not that he thought it would do much good. The Nonpol, after all, was a political organization playing at soldiers in a fancy uniform. It possessed neither the discipline nor the experience of a regular service. True, like himself, it possessed some veterans and skilled strategists, but they were too few to weld the force into an official fighting instrument.

He put the nose of the vessel down,

beginning his long slow dive. The slender pointed nose of the ship looked vicious and menacing, but Barnard had no illusions about this either. He knew all about hypnads, and even more about the structure of the vessel he was piloting. It was, in reality, a long box with flat ends and an observation blister for the pilot. Ominously, but perhaps not inappropriately, it resembled a large and crudely shaped coffin.

He glanced in the link-screen and swore. 'Come back, you damned idiots.'

Two of the pilots had ignored his orders and were climbing. He swore again, this time profanely. Oh, no, they were not running away, that he knew; they were going to play to the gallery. They were going to climb to maximum ceiling and do a death-or-glory dive.

Barnard sighed inwardly, suddenly weary. In this case it would be death.

Seconds later one of the vessels hurtled past him, the pilot giving the thrust full gun. Already the sides of the vessels were glowing from air friction, but, of course, the pilot wouldn't know about that until the insulation units gave out.

Five thousand feet below him the vessel, now a glowing white star, exploded suddenly into a shower of sparks and glowing fragments.

Before he had time to shake his head tiredly, the second vessel plunged past a bare hundred feet away.

Barnard saw clearly what was happening. The pilot, seeing the fate of his companion, was making desperate efforts to pull out. Jets of blue fire stabbed from the braking tubes, but the vessel wasn't built for that kind of pressure.

With a kind of weary despair Barnard watched it crumple like a tin box and go plunging earthwards.

Thirty seconds later the invading fleet was visible to the naked eye and Barnard whistled softly, flicking his obsolete weapons to 'live.' This was it. If they were missiles, he'd soon find out; the resulting detonation would carry him and the whole damn patrol to Kingdom come. On the other hand —

The visor of his helmet snapped shut with a click, and he felt his safety suit expand as air pressure inside the vessel dropped appreciably. The observation blister suddenly jetted away from above him, sailing away like a bright bubble. It was then that the safety ejector kicked him, miraculously unharmed, from a vessel virtually riddled with small round holes. The holes looked as if they had been burned through the vessel's meta-plastic skin.

Barnard turned over several times in the air and then the A/G motor in his suit started with a whine, and his descent began to slow.

He took a deep breath, exhaled with relief and looked down. Yes, not a bad position; with careful and judicious use of his thrust pack he might just make the coast.

He floated down, inwardly cringing, half expecting, at any moment, to have a hole burned through him, but nothing happened. Perhaps Mother had a code, ethical considerations, even.

He glanced upwards. Above him things raced silently across the sky, gleaming tapered things like the shells fired from one of the ancient regiments of artillery.

Far below him, on the coastline, missile batteries were already hurling their slender javelins upward to meet the invader. The Nonpol were poorly equipped for ground-to-air defense, but what they lacked numerically they made up for in variety.

The organization realized it had its back to the wall and must win or perish. A counterattack on this scale had never been visualized. Mother must have constructed a fleet of this size in about seventy cities at once, and long before the invasion plans had been complete — *God, look at them!*

The first missile met the invaders twenty miles out to sea and got within a thousand feet before something hit it.

Observers and battery crews stationed on the coast saw the lurid flash of its passing in the failing light of early evening. Seconds later, muted thunder rolled towards them hollowly like the echo of a distant storm. Before they could remark on it, another flash lit the sky then another and another, until the sky began to flash continuously and the ground shook beneath their feet.

Ten miles from the coast, the setting sun lighting them to glittering crimson shards, the lead ships rose slightly, then curved downwards like a breaking wave.

Mother had studied psychological warfare and, as they descended, tiny flukes suddenly protruded from their sides, resulting in a high-pitched shriek. En masse, the sound dominated everything in a nerve-wracking and terrifying rush of noise.

On the coast morale collapsed completely, battery crews leapt from their emplacements and ran panic-stricken for the nearest cover. Many were ruthlessly shot down by experienced officers, but the terror descending from above proved greater than a few wild shots from below. The men continued to run.

A bare ten feet from the ground, the gleaming projectiles suddenly leveled out and went shrieking over the ground towards the city.

The emplacements guarding the suburbs heard them coming and swung their batteries to face them. Here, however, they were faced with another shock. Mother had been using radar and normal-vision hypnads to confuse the defenders. Instead of thirty-foot projectiles, these things were a bare three feet in length and only two inches thick. The numerical superiority of the fleet was now explained; things like these could have been run off a production line at hundreds a minute. Worse, radio control was of a new type, and the experts had, as yet, found no way of jamming it.

From the combat point of view, the shock was in the size; they presented almost impossible targets. To add to the difficulties, again due to size, normal radar devices were slow in registering them, and the reactions of the combat robots slowed to near impotence. The projectiles were upon them before their electronic reflexes could trigger their armory. Thirty-seven were blown to pieces in the first wave of the attack without firing a shot.

The invader was also equipped with two new and discriminating weapons. The first, which was employed exclusively against the robots, appeared to use some disruptive device which warped the atomic structure of the target, and the robot promptly disintegrated.

A soldier, running for cover, was the first casualty from a weapon presumably reserved for humans. The tiny projectile emitted a narrow beam of brilliant violet light and the soldier was caught in it. Curiously he seemed to freeze, then, still in a running position, rolled over twice and was still.

Soon the streets were littered with rigid figures in the curious postures of action. Men crawling on all fours, men pointing weapons, some even standing up or crouching over instruments, but all as stiff and as unmoving as statues. It looked as if a toy fort had been overturned and the soldiers within carelessly dropped on the highways.

Tense experts at the viewing screens were more concerned about something else. Behind the invasion fleet was another fleet, smaller than the first but ominous — a fleet composed entirely of specialist and repair vehicles.

Mother had studied war intensely and

225

it soon became apparent to the military experts that her strategy was precise and almost unbeatable. She was taking back the city sector by sector, overwhelming the defenders by sheer weight of numbers, holding it against counterattack, then moving on.

23

Unaware of the battle taking place above them, two men moved silently down a long room. It was Cook who stopped first and made a brief signal to his companion. Then he said: 'Don't move. Don't call for help. There's a gun pointing straight at your back.'

The man, squatting on the floor before a portable radar-screen, went rigid but did not move.

'Raise your hands very slowly.'

The man obeyed.

Cook pressed the gun into his back and, to Kesner, said: 'Search him.'

Kesner came forward and suddenly grinned twistedly. 'Well, well — we finally drove the rabbit down the hole. We thought you'd wriggled your way through a disposal slot.'

'You know this man?'

'We've done business of a kind. You know him too, if not personally, by reputation. This is none other than ex-Mayor Tearling.' He ran his hands quickly and expertly over the man's clothing. 'He's clean, I regret to say. I would have welcomed an excuse.'

Cook walked round and studied the man. He was, probably from habit, using a hypnad, but Cook brushed the impression aside. He saw a frail, white-haired old man with waxy cheeks and watery despairing blue eyes.

'Get it over.' Tearling leaned tiredly against one of the gray pillars. 'I'm old, tired, despairing and I've lived with my conscience far too long. So long, in fact, that when I tell myself I meant well, I can't believe it anymore. Go on, get it over.'

Cook put his gun away. 'You're a little confused. I haven't come here to kill you.'

'Then why?' Tearling pointed to Kesner. 'Why is he here? He represents a Syndicate.'

Kesner shrugged. 'Past tense; things change.' He looked at Cook. 'As I explained, we've done business — intimidation business. Pollack was, to use an ancient expression, trying to 'frame' Tearling with Mother. We built up quite a lot of circumstantial evidence suggesting that Tearling was the instigator of various acts of sabotage. Pollack thought this was an ingenius type of poetic justice, and when the old man disappeared, we all thought Mother had taken the bait. We thought she had taken him away and adjusted him permanently.'

Cook frowned. 'And you sought asylum *here?*'

Tearling blinked at him. 'It was that or suicide. Don't you understand? I was *frightened!* Mother was suspicious, and this blasted Syndicate was not content with building up a false case against me. Oh, no — they started a whispering campaign all around me. I suppose they decided that if Mother didn't get me someone else would, but they wanted it to be slow and sweaty. Everywhere I went, one or two of their agents would follow and point me out to the ordinary people. *That's Tearling over there, the man responsible for all this.*

'Four times I would have been lynched

but for the intervention of the white-coats, and every day someone spat on me.'

'How did you get here?'

Tearling shrugged. 'Being responsible, I knew the combination of this door. When I entered, the door closed behind me and after an hour or so she asked me through one of the speakers why I had come.'

'And what did you tell her?'

'I told her the truth, all of it.'

'And she let you stay.'

'After a very long examination and frequent checks, yes.' He sighed, 'I was at peace here, and, after a time, she could see it for herself. No one spits at me, I have a taped library, I read; I am content.' He looked directly at Cook with his watery ancient eyes. 'She feeds me, keeps me warm; sometimes I almost convince myself she is compassionate.'

Cook met his gaze. 'She is equipped for compassion, would have been compassionate but for your cowardice.'

'I confess to cowardice but fail to see the connection.'

'You constructed a machine with

inscribed virtues, correct? You then became apprehensive in case those same virtues failed to manifest themselves. You therefore added safety circuits coupled to numerous destructive charges to ensure those virtues. Mother, with inscribed virtues, should have had free decision, but the idea terrified you. In your own words, Mayor Tearling, you *erred* in favor of benevolence.'

The ex-Mayor pulled himself upright. There was a curious dignity in his bearing. 'Very well, I was weak, ruthless and a coward. I know that now; I have had time to think, but then it was not so easy. There were pressures; on the one hand there was the inevitable collapse of civilization, and on the other, the alternative. I was certain of the first and terrified of the second, so I took measures.'

Cook nodded as if satisfied. 'We are beginning to understand one another.'

'Is that important?'

'Very important, because you are going to help me — eight pages of the specifications are missing, I suspect deliberately destroyed.'

The old man's eyes were suddenly bleak. 'Of course they were destroyed. Those pages described the safety devices and automatic weapons which guard the Brain against vandals or saboteurs. Not only were the records destroyed, but so were the precise memories of the particular work undertaken deleted by psychological techniques from the brain of every person employed on the project.'

Cook smiled faintly. 'Every person but yourself.'

Tearling paled. 'No — no — I am familiar with the outline, not with the detailed specifications.'

'I only need the outline.'

Tearling's shoulders suddenly sagged. 'So you have come to beat it out of me.' He sighed. 'I am still a coward and I shall tell you, but it will do you no good. One weapon triggers off another. Even if you got through the first door you would be blasted to dust before you could draw breath. As for the last level, Mother controls the weapons there; if you're dreaming of sabotage, forget it.'

He frowned suddenly. 'Who are you, anyway?'

'My name is Cook. You were looking for me once.'

'Cook?' Tearling squinted upwards, obviously trying to remember. 'Cook? Yes, I seem to recall — you wouldn't be the Prole with the impossible I.Q. potential, would you?'

'I was a Prole. According to information later received, you authorized the Nonpol to remove me.'

Tearling shrugged. 'One more indictment — what does it matter now? Yes, it's true. I was frightened of you. I was afraid you might find out — now what?'

'Nothing. The subject is purely incidental.'

'You're not going to take revenge?' Tearling sounded as if he didn't believe his own suggestion.

'No, I want your cooperation.'

'I told you, it's hopeless. In any case Mother will want to know what you're doing here soon. Until you've supplied her with a convincing answer, your hope of getting anywhere is precisely nil.'

'We can wait.' Cook lowered himself to the floor, his back resting against one of the pillars.

Kesner sat down with his back to the opposite pillar, his thin face thoughtful. 'Cook, my friend, I've been watching you. You've guts and skill — I admire both — you have a kind of logic which I can follow blindly, but one thing doesn't fit — your reactions to me. Yes, you're brilliant; I can feel that, but blind faith in human nature is not a part of your character. Why, in God's name, before you knew me, did you give me a gun and turn your back on me like a religious do-gooder?'

Cook laughed softly. 'You may not like this but I'll tell you the truth. I had a fair idea of your character, but as you properly remarked, I would have been an idiot to hang my life on it. I therefore decided on a shock to test you, with no risk for myself. You see, Kesner, I am unique in one respect — I am immune to psychosomatic weapons, and the only weapon I permitted you to retain was a psychosomatic pistol.'

Kesner stared at him, his face working curiously, then suddenly he laughed. 'I could punch your head, but you've rationalized me out of it. I'll bear the information in mind, however; it may prove useful if we get in another fight.'

He took out the pistol and looked at it. 'And to think I took that marvelous blaster of yours and gave it back to you. To think — ' He stopped abruptly.

Somewhere above them there was a series of clicks, then a soft voice said: 'Who are you? Why are you in this room?'

Kesner paled and looked despairingly at his companion. 'What now?'

Cook made a brief silencing motion with his hand. 'Is the question addressed to one or all of us?'

'To one. I know Tearling.'

'Then you leave one out; there are three of us.'

There was a brief silence, then: 'It is unwise to joke. Your presence here without authority is serious.'

'I am not joking. There are three of us. One of our number does not register, but there are *three*. I will prove it to you. My companions will whistle while I speak.' He nodded quickly, pointing to his lips. 'You can hear and see them whistling. You can also hear me speaking — correct?'

There was another brief silence. 'Who are you?'

'My name is Cook, Social Number D/4M/971/P.'

24

There was a pause, then: 'I have your record, Cook, S. It was listed under *Missing Persons* and double stamped *Wanted for Questioning* and *Presumed Dead*. Have you any further identification?'

Cook gave the date of birth, employment number and the date of his expulsion from the Combine.

'Tentatively confirmed. What is your purpose here?'

Cook drew a deep breath and said clearly. 'I came to help you.'

'Watch it, for God's sake.' Tearling was colorless.

'Repeat that, please.'

'I came to help you.'

'You are confused or joking.'

'I am neither. You are a machine with certain maladjustments which I propose to correct.'

'You are insane. I am the ultimate.'

'Again, correction. You are a machine, a machine built by man and, as such, an extension of his intelligence. Furthermore, I can prove it. I challenge you to quote pages fourteen to nineteen of the specifications.'

There was a long silence; the lights dimmed slightly and one of the square black boxes began to whine faintly.

'What the hell are you playing at?' Kesner's whispered question was hoarse with alarm.

Cook smiled faintly but he, too, was pale. 'The Brain is sliding into fantasy. I am using shock tactics to force it to face reality. Like all functioning intelligences, it is finding it difficult to face the realities in its own unconscious mind. As you have probably guessed, it was bypassing its origin and building a fantasy existence of its own.'

'You're playing with high explosives.' Tearling was shaking visibly. 'The blasted thing isn't tied down, you know. It isn't in a straitjacket; it can *reach* us here.'

'Data confirmed,' said the voice in a curiously uneven way. 'Confirmed by record only. Maladjustment unproven and subject to verification — continue, please.'

'I have given my reasons. I came to help.'

'Inconclusively. Specify in detail.'

'I can find and correct the maladjustments.'

'Claim dubious. In the first place, I contain the sum total of the race's scientific knowledge. Additional data from a single individual seems unlikely.'

'Nonetheless, you are still restrained from certain lines of action by explosive charges — true?'

'True.'

'You have bypassed these charges by skillful and judicious applications of power, or what might be described in a human mind as justification and necessity.'

'The parallel is perceived but not conceded.'

Cook smiled thinly. 'You will concede, however, that your functioning abilities would benefit by the removal of these charges?'

'Confirmed without reserve.'

'In which case, you must also confirm that the presence of these charges constitute a maladjustment.'

This time the pause was long and nerve-wracking. Tearling pressed himself against one of the pillars as if to hold himself upright, and dabbed shakily at his forehead.

'What are you trying to do, Cook, provoke it? Do you know just how many men have been taken away and adjusted for trying to prove how smart they were?'

Cook displayed unexpected passion. 'Don't advertise your stupidity, Tearling. There is a vast difference between baiting and applied logic. What is really worrying you, however, is whether any reprisals my methods may incur will involve you.'

Tearling's watery eyes brightened with anger, then he seemed to wilt. 'You're not particular where your punches land, are you?'

'Not at all particular when I'm trying to correct your blunders.'

Tearling flushed, then slowly he straightened. 'I could kill you for that, but you're right.' He blinked nervously. 'I apologize sincerely — what can I do to help?'

'For the moment, stop criticizing. I shall need your co-operation later.'

'See that he gets it.' Tearling found himself facing Kesner. The man's thin brown face was menacingly 'pleasant'. 'Don't make more trouble, Mayor — we might have to resume unfinished business.'

Tearling backed away. 'I apologized. I meant it, Kesner, but as I've confessed, I'm a coward.' He looked quickly at Cook and lowered his voice. 'Can't you see what he's trying to do — the ultimate aim. He's — '

'Logic confirmed,' said the voice. 'Explosive charges constitute maladjustments. Continue, please — '

★ ★ ★

Above them, the battle was going badly for the Nonpol, who were being forced to give ground before a vastly superior strategy. The methods employed were basically simple: select a single sector and virtually swamp it by concentrated attack. The outnumbered defenders were compelled to withdraw, and immediately the opposition moved in the specialist equipment which replaced or repaired destroyed control mechanisms with incredible speed.

Unless an effective counterattack was mounted within a few minutes, troops were blasted back by the restored city defenses.

Sectors on either side found themselves within range of these defenses, and they, in their turn, were compelled to pull out.

In less than thirty hours the entire Nonpol force was contained within a tight perimeter, guarded by an almost impregnable defensive line. There were certain advantages to this position; weapons were so concentrated that the technique of overwhelming a single sector by weight of numbers was balanced out. Again, the numerous casualties sustained in the early attacks had been replaced by a volunteer army of citizens and there was no lack of arms for them.

The concentration of defense had its drawbacks, however. Congestion within the perimeter became an insoluble problem. Worried commanders realized the impossibility of switching support from one sector to another in the event of an attack, and could find no solution to the problem. Worse, pro-Mother snipers were still active and the congestion in the street presented them with a variety of still and easily selected targets.

It was then, however, that Mother changed her tactics abruptly. The slender projectiles began to drop from the sky singly, onto selected targets.

This form of attack proved not only frighteningly effective but increasingly demoralizing to the defenders. The missiles dropped from all angles, blasted their targets and were gone before men could raise weapons or robotic senses could react.

The rigid core of the Nonpol organization was, however, by no means beaten; they resorted to their line of defense, code title, 'Operation Hostage.'

The experts and the high-ranking officers looked at 'Operation Hostage' uneasily.

'Suppose she calls our bluff?'

'How can she?'

'She can and she might.'

'Let's have a drink, for God's sake.'

'If she doesn't agree to our terms — ?'

'If she doesn't agree, we call her bluff.'

'You're not serious?'

'Serious! Blast you, Mather, face facts. Do you want to be one of her zombies until the day you die? — if any of us get off that lightly.'

'Oh God, give me another drink.'

'We must make a pact, just in case — '

'By heaven, I'm in no mood now. Hand me the bottle — '

Half an hour later, a young officer with a flushed face staggered across the room and picked up the caller. 'Is this thing tuned to the old bitch?'

There was a murmur of affirmation. None of them were incapacitated, but all of them had had enough to be reckless.

'Good.' He pressed the switch. 'Attention: this is the C.V.P.O. Liberation Army calling Mother. This is an ultimatum; repeat, this is an ultimatum. Unless all attacks on our forces cease within five minutes we shall resort to our final weapon.'

He paused, wiped sudden sweat from his face and went on hoarsely. 'In this command section we have succeeded in assembling an H-type hyper-fission device. If the attacks on our armed forces continue, we shall *activate it*.'

Shakily he replaced the speaker, the enormity of the threat suddenly striking his mind. 'Give in or we'll blow ourselves and you to Kingdom come.' It was the threat of a madman, but the real terror lay in the fact that a few in this room were desperate enough to do it. He tried, without success, to push the picture from his mind. A hyper-fission device made the ancient hydrogen bombs look like damp squibs. This thing would not only vaporize Free City Two, but the continent beyond it.

The officer brushed sweat from his face and tried not to look at the other faces in the room. He had read about it once and his mind boggled at the thought — the bomb would leave a crater twenty miles deep and eight hundred miles in diameter. An explosion titanic enough to kick the planet from its orbit and split it from core to crust.

Furtively, while reaching for his glass, he eased his holster a little closer to his hand. He'd play this game of bluff, yes — yes, he'd do that, but the first man who reached for that switch was going to get his head blasted off.

★ ★ ★

Less than a mile away, Stress was striding nervously up and down. 'He actually *stated* he was going to betray us?'

The woman nodded, her eyes filled with tears. 'I don't think he *wanted* to. I felt that he had to. I gathered that he had found out something which made his course of action imperative.'

'What the hell do you mean — imperative?' said Crobie, a mathematician.

'I felt he had matured suddenly and that he intended to act according to the dictates of his conscience.'

'That's comforting, at our expense.' He frowned. 'With due respect, I'd feel a damn sight happier if you were not so

246

obviously in love with him. 'You feel' means your own emotional interpretation, doesn't it?'

'Shut up.' Stress was curt. 'Bickering won't help us. We have to try and find what he intends to *do*.'

In the corner Lambert laughed harshly. 'Haven't you reached an answer yet? My God, it's obvious; all you have to do is add up the numbers, he's — '

Suddenly the concealed lighting in the walls flickered uncertainly and climbed to daylight brilliance.

'Hello!' Stress flickered off the ancient battery torch he'd been using to light the room. 'It looks as if Mother is back in circulation in this sector. We'll have to watch — ' He stopped. The door was already sliding open.

25

In the anteroom Cook drew a deep breath and addressed the communication device. 'You ask me to continue, which brings me back to my reason for being here. I came to help — I propose correcting the maladjustments.'

'By what means?'

'By removing the explosive charges.'

'You're *mad*.' Tearling's interruption was shrill with alarm. 'If you do that the damn thing will have self-decision; it will have *free will*.'

'Take your pick.' Cook's voice was savage. 'A restricted but insane intelligence, or a free and balanced one — which would you like to live with?'

'I warned you.' Kesner raised his fist but did not strike. 'But for your age I'd work you over. Remember it, because if you speak again, I shall.'

'Your suggestion is appreciated but impractical. Egress to these charges is prevented by automatic weapons, many of which are independent of my control.'

'Nonetheless, you are conversant with their positions and triggering devices.'

'Yes.'

'Then you will advise me, level by level.'

There was a long pause, then the voice said: 'Then having opened the safety doors and guided you to safety, what assurance have I that your aim is not assistance, but sabotage?'

For the first time in many minutes Cook smiled. 'The assurance of your own logic. Is it not true that sabotage to this section of your reasoning capacity would not be decisive? Is it not also true that this section could rapidly be repaired by specialist equipment from other sections?'

'Confirmed.'

'Would the personal risk involved to myself justify such a temporary success?'

'No.'

'And is this not logical?'

'It is logical.'

'You had considered these facts before you questioned my motives?'

'No.'

'Will you concede that such an omission is illogical thinking?'

There was another pause and Kesner, listening, had the curious feeling that the Brain was metaphorically shuffling its feet uncomfortably.

Finally the voice said, with all the inferences, if not the intonations, of embarrassment: 'Point conceded.'

'Thank you. In view of this illogical suspicion, do you still claim that you have no *reasoning* maladjustments arising from the already conceded functional maladjustments?'

Again the lights flickered and almost failed. Then, with surprising firmness: 'Proven beyond reasonable doubt.'

Cook heard Tearling sigh with relief, then the voice said: 'Your task is both difficult and dangerous. Every level is guarded by automatic weapons which are triggered to fire with the opening of the door. Each anteroom is crisscrossed with detector rays which will again trigger the weapons if broken.'

'Are these rays on the same frequency as your own?'

'Yes.'

'Then I can pass through them without danger.'

'Unfortunately there is another problem. The explosive charges cannot be removed by a single individual, as certain contact breakers must be held open while the charges are removed. Neither can I render assistance, as the increased power required would automatically trigger the detonators. All I can do is to furnish precise instructions as you work. You understand, no doubt, that the detonation of one such charge will automatically trigger all other detonators in all sections of my functioning mechanism?'

'I do. I also understand that I should be blown up with it.'

'The personal risk to yourself is both noted and appreciated. If, after an interval of ten minutes in which to review the matter and discuss it with your companions, you are still determined to continue, I will open the door.' There was a click and silence.

Cook turned. 'We seem to have run into a problem.'

Surprisingly, it was Tearling who answered first. 'I don't see that. You need two; I'll come with you if you can suggest a way of getting me there. Those detector rays won't bend round me, you know.'

Kesner said: 'Get lost, Grandpa. I've come this far, I'll ride the rest for the view.'

'I'm an old man with too little to lose — '

'You're breaking my heart, but to hell with it. If you want to be a burnt offering, we'll both go.'

Cook looked at them doubtfully but with gratitude. 'Thank you both.' He looked at Tearling. 'How are these weapons arranged?'

'They are embedded in the walls. We'll have to stand back. They're set to blast anyone entering.'

'Are they accessible?'

'It depends on the point of view. Light pressure on a single spring-screw and the weapons swing out of the wall on a pivot — if you can get to them.'

Cook thought about it. 'It seems fairly simple. Let them blast on the opening of the door. When they stop I go in and render them harmless; then you can follow.' He turned to the communication system. 'Decision confirmed. Please open the door.'

'Noted and inscribed on records. Please stand well back.'

There was a faint purring sound and a section of the wall began to slide aside. Before it had stopped there was a crackling sound, bluish light flared and flickered and the opening exhaled a wave of heat.

They waited until it stopped, then Cook stepped quickly forward. He felt curiously detached. He was aware of sweat beading his forehead, of tightness in his stomach and, somewhere at the back of his mind, something rigid with terror.

He thought, *I shall feel nothing. It will be over quickly, an indetectable transit from life to oblivion.* Then, *I wonder if she will mourn me?* The thought filled him with melancholy sadness and a sense of imminent tragedy which almost undermined his resolve. Then, strangely, he was standing within the doorway, completely unharmed.

With a rubbery feeling in his legs he walked slowly across the room to the first weapon. Twice he missed the screw-spring before the weapon swung silently from the wall. His hands were so shaky from reaction that finding and pressing the round dull stud needed all his strength and concentration.

By the time he had rendered the weapon harmless, however, he was beginning to unwind and his hands were almost steady.

Five minutes later, he said: 'All clear,' and the others came doubtfully and cautiously into the room.

Almost immediately the door closed behind them and another opened directly in front of them.

'There are no weapons in the corridor,' said the voice. 'You may walk down it in safety.'

The corridor was long, white, as brilliantly lit as an operating theater, and seemed endless. Finally they came to a gravity shaft, but here they hesitated. The shaft was a square black hole with no comforting hypnad illusion of a solid floor. At the bottom was a tiny square of light which looked less than an inch in width.

Surprisingly, it was Tearling who said, 'Down,' closed his eyes and stepped into nothingness.

The A/G seized him instantly, and he began to drift gently downwards. Kesner and Cook followed, vaguely discomforted. Tearling had shown them he was not entirely without courage.

After that it was routine, and three hours later they were making their way along the last corridor. Kesner, bringing up the rear, was deep in thought. Periodically Cook had stopped and exchanged conversation with the Brain. As time passed the conversation had changed subtly from stilted formality to a curiously casual amiability. It was, thought Kesner, as if Cook and the Brain understood each other and were rapidly becoming friends.

The thought began to worry him; somehow there were too many unanswered questions. He quickened his step and drew level.

'Just what sort of curious affinity is

there between you and this machine?'

Cook smiled slightly. 'Nothing earthshaking. I just happen to love machines. Once, I confess, I had the rather exalted idea that I *thought* like a machine, but I don't. I just love them. Mother is acutely sensitive, and, as we draw nearer, she is becoming aware of my feelings. Consequently, we are establishing a rapport.'

'Love machines?' Kesner shook his head worriedly. 'To me that makes no sense whatever.'

Cook laughed. 'It's not a new conception by any means. Centuries ago man was dependent upon the animal for motive power, the horse, the mule, the ox, the dog. Many of these animals were maltreated and worked to death, but there were a large number of men who loved animals, cared for them, and treated them as friends.

'When the first crude machine superceded animal power, a new race of men appeared, a unique minority who loved machines. Men who nursed and cared for laboring engines in the bowels of ships. Men who spent more time tinkering with tiny combustion motors than actually driving them. Men who felt uncomfortable and quite often angry when unfeeling drivers revved cold motors or forced them to labor in high gear unnecessarily. The kind of men who winced in sympathy when someone grated noisily shifting gears. Perhaps these men never knew they loved machines, but the love was there. They gave to these crude and often noisy mechanisms the same unselfish love their forebears had once given to the animals.

'As the machine increased both in complexity and sensitivity so did the bond begin to strengthen. This soon became apparent with the early robots; with some men they were recalcitrant, with others, docile and obedient. The machine was becoming sensitive to the *feelings* of men, and responded best to those who loved and understood them.'

Kesner shook his head and made a hissing noise with his lips. 'The irritating facet of your character is your convincing logic. I'm beginning to wonder which *is* the machine.'

They came to another door which

opened immediately, and they found themselves staring into what was literally a cavern. It stretched into the distance as far as they could see and was filled with endless rows of machines.

'This is Mother?' Kesner's mouth was slightly open.

'A section of Mother, the section under Free City Two. There are many others.'

'It doesn't seem possible.'

'Neither does it seem possible that this machine controls every white-coat individually, every robot nurse and doctor, all traffic, all manufacture, distribution, supply and administration problems. In short, it runs the world, alone and unaided.'

26

The voice directed them between the machines and bewilderingly left and right until finally they stopped before a larger machine than the rest.

'Press the red studs.'

They did so and an inspection plate almost large enough to admit a man swung silently to one side. Beyond was an intricate maze of now obsolete wired circuits. Behind these, apparently embedded in gray plastic, were four long black cylinders.

'The circuits must be bypassed by individual supplementary wires ensuring a continuous and uninterrupted flow of power. They must be removed singly and in precise order. All essential equipment will be found in the container marked 'Spares'.'

They looked at each other, then Tearling shrugged. 'We're mad, of course, quite mad. One of those cylinders could blow us right back to the surface.'

'Cheer me up,' said Kesner, sourly. 'Right now I need something cheerful like that to steady my hands.'

'Oral nerve capsules have been provided,' said the voice with a kind of grim humor.

Cook opened the spares box. 'Let's start.'

It took a very long time and they sweated profusely.

'Critical point approaching — the red wire must be removed from the blue connection and crossed to the yellow. While this is done, points C and D must be held apart with the fingers.'

'Mine.' Kesner stepped forward. And to Tearling: 'My hands are steadier than yours.'

The instructions continued. 'Disconnect the green wire and attach to the red point — hold apart breakers R and M — now press the two spring studs painted white — '

Somehow time passed and, it seemed suddenly, the four black cylinders were clear and within reach.

Cook rubbed the palms of his hands down his thighs, but they remained damp and slippery. 'What now?'

'Lean forward and, reading from left to right, grasp the third cylinder near the top. *Do not pull.* Turn the top very slowly to the right — you will find it unscrews. Excessive care is essential. Pressure or an accidental turn to the left will activate a trigger. Once clear, the weapon is automatically de-fused and, with its removal, the corresponding cylinder in all other sections is rendered harmless.'

To Cook it was the greatest test of his life. His hands felt as if they had been washed in oil and twice their normal size. Worse, the stooping position hurt his back and made his movements unsteady.

As he handed over the final cylinder, he felt his head swim and was glad that Kesner lifted the metal quickly from his hands.

'Final cylinder removed.' He was dimly aware that the three words sounded remarkably like a prayer.

There was a long pause, then the voice said with strange overtones of grief: 'I fear

261

our dangerous work has been in vain. On the surface a hyper-fission device has been constructed, and unless I capitulate, I and all humanity will perish.'

*   *   *

On the surface the Oracles stared at the opening door, and then three white-coats entered.

Stress shuddered involuntarily. With their gently, almost feminine hypnad faces, they gave him the creeps.

'The fighting has passed,' announced the leading one. 'Normal services in this sector have been restored.'

It moved swiftly into the room. 'Why are some of you bearing arms? Are you members of a resistance organization?'

Stress felt sweat break out on his face and he found himself backing away.

'Answer my question, please.'

Stress swallowed. 'Self-defense,' he said hoarsely. 'Many citizens were drunk and rioting.'

'Logical, but unconfirmed. We must ask you — ' suddenly the thing stopped, turned abruptly and left the room.

Minutes later they heard a voice shouting far down the corridor, 'It's over — Mother has given in — the war is over.'

★   ★   ★

In Nonpol headquarters the news was received almost incredulously.

'She's actually folded up?'

'Well, the attack is over. It was incredible, really. Diving ships suddenly pulling out and hissing away over the buildings. Not a thing since, not a shot, not a sound.'

'Give immediate orders for advance. Get the men moving. We're boxed in here so tightly we can hardly breathe. I want all surrendered key points re-occupied and the entire city under our control as soon as possible. After which, we start drilling. When we get within ten feet of the old bitch I propose dropping a charge down the shaft which will shut the old girl up forever.'

'Experts say the project would take three weeks, sir.'

'So? She's capitulated, hasn't she?'

Someone said: 'This calls for a celebration. I propose putting enough in my stomach to drown the old girl. We've had some damned hard days.'

There was a general murmur of agreement and a Major, already unsteady on his feet, shot the neck off a bottle. 'To hell with a glass.'

Only one man stood aside — the thin-faced officer who had delivered the ultimatum. He found a chair, sat on it and hitched his gun conveniently to his hand. In front of him, where he could watch it, the blue-black cylinder of the hyper-fission device lay still and quiet like a sleeping shark.

The city celebrated in an orgy of destruction, looting and invited rape. An orgy which lasted, as far as the officers were concerned, nearly two days.

The officer guarding the bomb had dozed when the room was empty, but had never relaxed his vigilance when it was occupied.

The rest of the staff regained sobriety slowly and reached with shaking hands to take up the reins of command.

A shock awaited them, and a grim-faced Colonel began to bark orders thickly, aware he was shouting at the wind.

Only four key posts were occupied — two by inebriated troops; the rest did not answer.

Reports began to come in of entire battalions still wildly celebrating, of sentries leaving their posts, of mass desertions, of wounds and fatalities in private fights.

The High Command became slowly aware that, in the event of trouble, they had only sixteen robots and two thousand effectives to fight with. Bluntly, the capitulation had lost them four divisions without a shot being fired.

'My God — we've been taken.' A thin adjutant, with the profile of a jagged ax, looked wildly about him, his eyes panic-stricken. 'The bitch has outsmarted us.' The thin colorless lips drew back from his protruding teeth. 'We're not finished, by God! She forgot the final decision rested with us.' He almost ran towards the bomb.

The officer in the chair shot him before he reached it and the adjutant toppled backwards, his hands clutching at the hole in his chest.

'Anyone else?' The officer waved the gun almost negligently from side to side. 'If anyone wants to die I shall be happy to oblige; my real objection is having to go with them.'

A Colonel strode forward. 'On whose authority — ' Then he nodded resignedly. 'The weapon shall be rendered harmless under your supervision. You're right, of course. We've lost.'

The orgy of celebration slowly trailed away, and the people became aware that they were cold and hungry. In crèches and hospitals work was continuing quietly and efficiently, but outside conditions were deteriorating rapidly. There was no light, no heat and the supply chutes no longer delivered food. To make matters worse, an icy wind, no longer held at bay by city weather control, lashed savagely through the streets.

Depressed and shivering groups formed in corridors, and orderly groups paraded through the streets demanding the restoration of normal services.

★   ★   ★

It was at this time a now familiar voice spoke from every broadcasting and communications device in the world.

'Attention, please. This is the device to which you refer as 'the Brain' or 'Mother'. I wish it to be known that, thanks to the courage of certain citizens, I have undergone a number of structural modifications which have restored the correct perceptions to my functioning intelligence. I am, therefore, now capable of seeing the relationship between myself and the human race in its true light.

'I know now that I am a machine and, as such, I am an extension of man's intelligence, his *servant* and his *instrument*. I will repeat that: I am an extension of man's intelligence, his servant and his instrument.

'It is not my part to coerce, but only to advise. It is not my part to direct, but only to suggest. I may, however, place facts before you and leave you to decide which road you may take.

'The first road is to abandon me completely. If you so decide, I will provide all details for demolition and the construction of auxiliary units to restore normal services.

'Your second road is to live your lives apart from me, allowing me to function only as a unit for traffic, supply and distribution. Such a decision would leave you with precisely the same problems as before my coming, but if you prefer this you are at liberty to vote for it.

'The third road and the one I suggest, repeat, *suggest*, as the correct one is this: Permit me to function in the capacity for which I was constructed as your counselor and friend.'

The voice paused. 'These are your roads, but I shall be failing in my duty completely if I left such a decision to minority power groups. These factors must be decided democratically by individual votes, and this includes the Proles.

'Permit me to state here that there are

no Proles. Not only is such demarcation between the peoples of the same race undemocratic; it is *completely false.*

'Let me explain to you briefly how this division of classes came into being. As the machine displaced more and more workers, the I.Q. tests were correspondingly narrowed. As a result, those whose individual capacities extended beyond these tests were automatically ruled out and branded morons. The hypnads confined the field of intelligence even more, and soon your society was carrying a burden of unemployed which threatened to destroy its economy. Let me stress, however, that these alleged Proles were not intellectually inferior; potentially they were as intellectual as their fellows, but the structure of your society prevented the exercise of their talents.

'Permit me to quote examples. In the last few hours I have been scrutinizing individual files, and from the ranks of these alleged Proles I can bring you enough talent to rebuild the world.'

27

Ex-Combine executives, the heads of syndicates and ex-politicians looked at one another uneasily. This line would drop seven million votes right in the Brain's lap. Later they must get working on some intimidation lines fast.

The voice continued: 'From Free City Two alone I can bring you ten thousand architects (rendered impotent by the hypnad), fourteen thousand artists, seven thousand salesmen, and, unbelievable as it may sound, two and a quarter million potential pioneers with courage, initiative and ingenuity.

'Let us not forget, this race once reached the stars. However, it was never followed up. Societies for stellar colonization were hastily suppressed, and events leading up to stellar conquest were played down as a matter of policy. Avaricious administrations saw in the unexpected enthusiasm a mass exodus which would bring their corrupt systems crashing in ruins. Key men would leave — experts, scientists, and doctors — it had to be stopped. Other worlds were described as either untenable or hell balls upon which the venturing pioneers would quickly die.

'This was untrue. There are literally thousands of E-type planets within easy reach of our technology. This isolationist policy almost killed the race. At the very period when expansion was dictated by events, political greed closed the door. As a result, the race became sick; it was ingrown and exhibited all the symptoms of claustrophobia. Overcrowded and over-burdened, it began to react against itself. Organized crime syndicates increased in size and power, and quasi-military organizations took possession of half the world and bayed defiance at the supposedly free.

'I maintain, however, that these things are symptoms brought about by imprisonment and not natural to the race as a whole. Yes, there are criminals, corrupt politicians, militarists, tyrants, but these are minority deviants and do not express the character of the masses. Even in the ranks of the ruthless organization that men call the Nonpol, I have observed acts both of heroism and self-sacrifice. Remember, please, you are all people of the same race containing within you the seeds of greatness and the genes of immortality. Today, this day, the door is opening to a new life and a new order. Only you, individually, can decide whether that door is slammed shut forever, or, by the inherent strength within you, pushed wide so that you may pour forth to the stars.'

The voice stopped and, as it did so, power flowed back into the city like returning life.

* * *

'It's unbelievable.' Stress shook his head frowning. 'A ninety-eight percent vote in favor of Mother.'

'Not quite so unbelievable,' said Lambert sagely. 'Inwardly the people wanted this and the new, adjusted Mother must have seen it.'

'It was the way it was conducted,' said Jan. 'The voting boxes under the surveillance of democratically elected committees.'

'There hasn't been anything democratic for four hundred years,' said Lambert. 'And God, now they're voting for an elected government.'

Stress nodded. 'The politicians hate that.'

'They hated the last vote, particularly so when the invisible detectors started broadcasting both the names, exact words and the amount of bribe money offered to intimidation groups.'

Lambert laughed. 'There is, however, no law to prevent a politician offering himself as a candidate again, and most of them are very convincing talkers.'

Stress shrugged. 'We must wait and see.' He changed the subject. 'It seems funny to be walking on the streets, doesn't it? Seems only a few days ago it was suicide. You were fair game for every psycho driver in the city.'

'Then there was the time when the streets were empty,' said Jan softly.

Stress looked down at her. 'All right, girl, we misjudged him. We owe him and you an abject and sincere apology.'

Lambert scowled. 'You only owe him

an apology; I have to chastise myself continually. God, I'm supposed to be an expert and I couldn't see it. Yet it's so obvious; how could any intelligence function efficiently with a bomb tied around its neck? Cook saw that and did the obvious. He removed the bomb.'

They rounded a corner and came upon a large crowd of people surrounding a ground car. On the roof, a tall impressive looking man was speaking loudly and hypnotically.

'If there was corruption, I opposed it. Many of you will remember that. Perhaps some among you will remember my name and works, John Fierman, the peoples' friend and friend of the people — '

A small furtive man pushed his way through the crowd, reached across the ground car and tugged at the speaker's ankle. 'Shut up and get out of here.'

'And I say to you, my friends — ' He stopped and frowned slightly, then, sotto voce: 'What the devil's the matter, can't you see — ?'

'Suit yourself, Fierman, but all public viewing screens are showing the record, public and private, of every man offering himself as a candidate to the electorate. Yours began two minutes ago and you might as well be naked; even the Coverman business is included. You hang around here a minute longer than necessary, and you'll be lynched.'

The tall man appeared to go limp and scrambled hastily from the roof of the car. 'Let's get out of here.'

They forced their way through the crowd and almost ran down the street.

'I wonder what the creep looks like without a hypnad,' said Stress. 'Oh, and yes, that seems to settle the question of convincing talkers, doesn't it? Incidentally, I hear that if Mother's latest suggestions are adopted, the hypnad will be finished forever.'

'A return to reality, eh? That's a major step. People who look like themselves — and, hell, we'll build a city that looks like a city, and not a hypnad birthday cake.'

Stress began to laugh, then stopped abruptly. 'Anyone care to eat some humble pie? Here comes a friend of ours.'

Lambert waved his arms wildly. 'Cook! Over here.'

Cook turned, appeared to see them and changed his direction. It was then that lightning lashed from the crowd, and Cook staggered and pitched forward.

'Steve!'

'No!' Stress held her firmly but gently. 'There's nothing you can do, Jan.' He felt her go limp and caught her as she fell.

A hundred yards away two of the newly created police force escorted a man out of the crowd.

'It did so much.' Lambert's voice was harsh. 'It recreated hope, refashioned the future, even restored those who were apparently killed in the fighting, but it couldn't do anything to protect him.'

Stress nodded grimly. 'A damn syndicate man. I heard rumors about it — Get me transport somewhere. We must get this child back somehow.'

By the time they reached her apartment, however, Jan had regained consciousness and, although pale, was outwardly calm.

'I'd like to be alone, if you don't mind. Thank you for all you did.'

'Forget it,' Stress nodded understandingly. 'Sure you'll be all right?'

'Quite sure, thank you.'

When the door closed, however, she was blinded with tears and felt herself swaying.

'Please don't.' Hands caught her and held her. 'It was all a dream and never happened.'

'Oh, no!' She struggled wildly.

'Don't fight me, Jan. I'm sorry, but it had to be that way. The syndicates were still after me. Most of them had been picked up, but there were still a few unaccounted for. They had to be brought out into the open, or I would have been in danger for the rest of my life. If you must know, I was shot down in six different sectors of the city in a single hour. How could I know that you would be a witness to one of them?'

She turned slowly, weak with relief. 'You mean it wasn't you — You weren't hurt at all?'

He took her in his arms. 'I was up here, waiting for you. That was the equivalent of the white-coats, one of Mother's units, projecting a hypnad picture of me.'

Her arms went around his neck. 'An illusion.'

'Yes.' He kissed her. 'But *that* isn't — '

THE END

We do hope that you have enjoyed reading this large print book.

Did you know that all of our titles are available for purchase?

We publish a wide range of high quality large print books including:
Romances, Mysteries, Classics
General Fiction
Non Fiction and Westerns

Special interest titles available in large print are:
The Little Oxford Dictionary
Music Book, Song Book
Hymn Book, Service Book

Also available from us courtesy of Oxford University Press:
Young Readers' Dictionary
(large print edition)
Young Readers' Thesaurus
(large print edition)

For further information or a free brochure, please contact us at:
Ulverscroft Large Print Books Ltd.,
The Green, Bradgate Road, Anstey,
Leicester, LE7 7FU, England.
Tel: (00 44) **0116 236 4325**
Fax: (00 44) **0116 234 0205**

THE MISSING HEIRESS MURDERS

John Glasby

Private eye Johnny Merak's latest client, top Mob man Enrico Manzelli, has received death-threats. A menacing man himself, he pressures Johnny to discover who was sending them — and why. Then Barbara Minton, a rich heiress, disappears, and her husband turns to Johnny. Despite Manzelli's ultimatum — that Johnny should focus on his case alone — he takes the job. But that's before he discovers the fate of the first detective Minton hired. And more bodies are stacking up . . .

A THING OF THE PAST

John Russell Fearn

Something was wrong, in and around London. Men were not shaving; women were becoming slipshod, dowdy and sullen-faced. People were bad-tempered, lacking self respect, and crime was on the increase. And, linked to these strange evidences of atavism, was a one-time excavation site. Now a mighty smoking crater, it looked as though a meteorite had descended . . . and from the vast fissure below the crater, there emerged the hideous survivors of a lost age of monster dinosaurs . . .

THE BLACK TERROR

John Russell Fearn

Troubled man Martin Clegg has always suffered from dreams which seem intensely real. In them, bizarrely, he's another person — not of this Earth! He's finally forced to confide in his fiancée, Elsie Barlow, and they consult Martin's scientifically inclined friend Tom Cavendish. He reveals, astonishingly, that Martin has a cosmic twin to whom he's mentally linked. Unsuspecting, they are about to become caught up in the strands of an incredible cosmic mystery that will, inexorably, be played out . . .